BLACK REIGN II

Also by
Edd McNair

My Time to Shine

BLACK REIGN II

EDD MCNAIR

www.urbanbooks.net

Urban Books LLC
1199 Straight Path
West Babylon, NY 11704

ISBN-13: 978-1-60162-058-3
ISBN-10: 1-60162-058-6

First Mass Market Printing July 2008
Printed in the United States of America

10 9 8 7 6 5 4 3 2 1

Submit Wholesale Orders to:
Kensington Publishing Corp.
C/O Penguin Group (USA) Inc.
Attention: Order Processing
405 Murray Hill Parkway
East Rutherford, NJ 07073-2316
Phone: 1-800-526-0275
Fax: 1-800-227-9604

BLACK REIGN II

PART II

BLACK'S RETURN

Chapter One

"**O**utta this muthafucka. After four years of this solitude shit and livin' in this big-ass jungle, it's time for me to carry my ass." Black stared at himself in the mirror with a feeling of satisfaction inside—JB's facial expression as those two "nines" exploded in his face was all he needed to get back. "Who in the hell would of ever thought I'd catch that bitch nigga comin' out of Junior's, of all places? I been hustlin' these triflin'-ass boroughs, from Uptown to Brooklyn to Queens, for years and had no idea when I'd come across this nigga."

The nine shots to the head were strictly for Junie.

That muthafucka had no reason in the world to leave my brother on the side of the road with two in his head. He didn't live like that and he didn't deserve it.

"But I got him, Junie, and he knew it was me." Black's eyes watered from his past haunting him again.

* * *

Four years ago when he left, he left VA knowing the consequences if he stayed. (That Saturday night when Boot got killed and the Feds came kicking in doors kept playing over in his head.) With his crew in custody, he had only one choice: burst.

He was happy as hell when he saw Poppa pumping gas at the Exxon after all that shit kicked off. He hadn't seen Poppa in about five years—he'd been doing a bid for a malicious wounding charge.

Black had looked out for Poppa a couple times before he got locked, but nothing that would make him feel Poppa owed him anything.

He came up on Poppa and they embraced. "What the deal, Black?"

"Mad shit, kid."

"Heard you the fuckin' man, son. We catch all that shit Upstate."

"Well, did you catch when the Feds were comin' . . . because you should of called me? Shit just fell. They made a sweep and everybody fell." Black had a spaced-out look on his face. He was lost. No Dee, no Lo, no Junie, no moms.

"Whatever you need, son," Poppa said with a serious look on his face.

"I need you to get me the fuck up out of here— Philly, Jersey, New York—it don't matter."

"I don't have a car. This my mom's shit, and I only been home three days, Black. I don't even suppose to be leavin' the state."

"Fuck all that gay shit, Poppa. You still that same hungry-ass, young nigga that just came home and need some dough. What you gonna do? Check it— all I can offer right now is this Rolex and bracelet;

after you drop me off, you can have the whip."
Black knew he'd just made the right offer.

Poppa looked at the Integra and the jewels and
knew he had no choice. The jewels, he could off
and get dough to get on his feet, and the Acura
Integra with the stash box was a blessing in dis-
guise. Not only was this going to be a come up, but
somebody had to step up and handle Black's business in his absence. "Drop you off and I'm out,
Black."

"Let's go, son. We got to get the fuck outta here."
Black wanted to get to New York, where he knew it
would be impossible for him to be found.

Most niggas who got in trouble went to New
York, but usually ended up back in VA because
they couldn't cope with the streets in the big city.
But that was Black's last worry. He was a hustler
and he knew he could hustle any muthafuckin'
where. Nobody wa'n' gonna tell him he couldn't
get no money. He was built for this shit.

Poppa dropped his mom's car off and, without
a word, jumped in with Black and headed for
Interstate 264.

They reached Richmond and veered off on 95N;
they both knew the Chesapeake Bay Bridge was a
no-no for a fugitive.

Black sat back with no facial expression. His
whole life was over in a flash. He had to build
anew.

Poppa dropped Black off and gave him a number. "You can always reach me here. Black, I promise
you, nobody will ever know you saw me, or what's
goin' on. I'll let you know everything that's goin'
on in VA. Just call." Poppa prayed that Black would
remember this. That would be his ace in the hole.

"All right, Poppa. You are my only connect to VA. Hold me down." Black got out the car in front of the old two-story home.

They gave each other a pound, and Poppa was out, headed back to VA.

Black walked up to the door. It had been a while. But these were his peoples, so he knocked.

His cousin, Leeta, opened the door. "What you doin' here, Black?" She opened the door and hugged him. She knew from going down South to visit with her crew that her cousin was the man and all she had to do was say his name and it opened doors. She knew too he didn't fuck with New York. If he came in town it was always to Brooklyn and they would only get a phone call.

Now he was in Hollis, Queens and she knew something was up even though he came across as a laid-low type nigga without a lot to say.

"Who's that at the door, Leeta?" Her dad came down the stairs and pulled the door open some more. "Boy, come on in here." He pulled Black in. "Edna," he yelled to his wife of forty-five years, "fix the basement. Earl boy here from Virginia."

"How long he gonna stay?"

Shac looked at Black, looked into his eyes, looked outside and saw no car, looked at the floor and saw no bags.

"About as long as his daddy did when he came here in a hurry many years back." His voice faded up the stairs. Shac knew the scenario—get in trouble down South; run up North till shit die down.

"Nobody's to know I'm here, Leeta." Black looked at his cousin.

"A'ight, I know you done fuck up. What you do? You can tell me." She smiled at Black. All she really wanted to know was how long he was going to stick around because she knew all he needed was a guide around Queens, and this VA nigga could get it.

She knew he was still a fuck-up, and all the bad things they said that the other side of her family was into, but it made no difference to her, she looked up to that shit.

"So where Curtis? He still hustlin'?"

"He do . . . a little bit, but he workin' some job now too. But he can still put you in."

Black hadn't been in Queens a week when he decided JB had to go. Even though he was his main supplier for years, all ties were broken. Things were bad, and the only way they could be corrected was "somebody had to be outlined in chalk."

He knew JB always visited his sister, Jacqueline, and remembered Junie saying where she lived. The rest wasn't hard—she was still driving the same BMW.

He followed her into her building and raced up the flight of stairs, waiting on her as she waited on the slow elevator. She never noticed him as he slid past her in the black hoody.

She entered her apartment and before she could shut the door, Black forced his way in quickly.

She jumped back and reached in her purse, but Black busted her in the head with the butt of the gun.

She dropped everything and stood there, only the wall holding her up. "I don't know what's goin' on, Black. I don't get in my brother's affairs."

"Bitch, my brother dead and that's all you can

come up with. Fuck is you sayin'? He walked closer to her and caught her with a left jab that put her head through the plaster and a right uppercut that laid her ass out.

Darkness hit her.

When she came to, she was laying flat on her stomach, butt-naked with her hands and feet duct-taped.

She turned her head to see Black sitting in the chair holding an iron. He plugged it in.

She began to squirm and tears began to flow. It wasn't much more she could do with the rag in her mouth.

He turned the iron on high, sat it down, and walked over to her. He rubbed her hair and looked down at her. "I need to know two things: your brother's phone number and where he lives." Black moved the rag from her mouth.

"His number is 718-555-4444, and all I know is he lives in Manhattan," she said, talking fast.

"I just wanted to see if you were goin' to lie, and you did. Don't forget I know all that," he said, not really knowing.

"I'm sorry," she said through breaths. "I'll tell you."

"Too late, girlfriend." Black stuffed the rag deeper into her mouth. He turned up her stereo then he picked up the iron and snatched it out the wall. He took the extension cord and began to whip her as if she was a child.

She cried, and her body jumped with every forceful swing that cut her skin as he let out his immediate frustrations on this bitch that got his brother caught the fuck up.

"You thought this shit was a game. You thought

your brother had this shit all on lock." He grabbed her feet, flipped her over, and placed the iron in the crease of her pubic hair. Right where her legs came together. "I hope you recognize right from wrong in your next life, and wherever you end up—heaven or hell—tell 'em, 'Don't fuck with Black, that nigga from The Lakes.'"

Her body jolted from the pain. He let the iron go as the foul odor of burnt flesh and her body losing control hit him in the face. He reached for the belt she had and wrapped it around her neck and pulled tightly as her wiggles slowed and her body went limp.

Now JB will feel the pain for the rest of his life, just like me. Black eased out of the apartment.

A year and a half had passed and making money in Queens was for real. Curtis had gotten killed, and Black caught two bodies, trying to survive in the game. He was used to the killings and the murders, but this borough they call Queens was a miniature DC. Niggas was dropping like flies, and he really couldn't see why . . . because they wa'n' gettin' it like that.

After that second body he left Queens, and made his way over to his Uncle Les in Harlem. Living Uptown was like no other place. Harlem was wild and took no "shorts." Cats were organized. They made paper up and down Lennox and 7th Avenue like it was a real business. Black eased in and found work—Les had put him in with some cats as his nephew—but he was still a nobody and that's how he was getting paid.

He was a lookout for a while and thought niggas

might give him a chance, but he soon realized that if these cats didn't know you since P.S. 180 you got nowhere. So he waited for the right opportunity, and his role went back to stickup kid.

Stickup quickly became murder.

Black quickly burst from Harlem, feeling like New York was closing in on him. He left so fast, he never knew that his Uncle Les paid for his bodies with his life.

Black ended up in Wilmington, DE, playing the streets, fucking with the strip clubs, and seeing the money potential in this new town.

This is where he ran into Polite. (Polite was in the car with his cousin Curtis when they got shot up.) He was in a wheelchair now, in Wilmington, doing his thing.

Polite had a spot over in Roosevelt Projects in Brooklyn. He ran with a team of niggas that had several blocks locked. He and Black clicked, and Black became his legs. He told Black, "After that bullshit, I'm only fuckin' with my peoples from Brooklyn."

Black stayed in Brooklyn and earned the ranks of lieutenant, only reporting to Polite. Polite tried to make him a soldier in the organization, but Black quickly let him know he only killed if he wanted a nigga dead, not because the next nigga was too scared to put in work. Polite understood.

Polite was moving much weight in Brooklyn and Wilmington. Life was all right, but the bulk of his money didn't come from drugs.

Before the drugs, it was credit cards and checks.

Not personal checks, but company checks and company credit cards. Since they moved easier down South, Polite would send Black down to NC and SC to work the credit cards and check scams.

The idea was to get bitches to use the cards. As long as the card was signed on the back, they wasn't supposed to ask for ID. Buy from one store and return to another. Company checks were deposited. A seven-grand check would clear three grand in three days and the rest two days later. This money was always good, and this was when you got your gear right.

Polite had a gold mine in Wilmington, and Black was part of it. Whipping a 2001 GS400, Black was living well, but wasn't where he wanted to be. So he began to call Poppa. Poppa would meet him in Raleigh when he went down for other business so he could kill two birds with one stone. Black would give him a brick and he would pay next time around.

Poppa knew the day would come. He'd been keeping Black abreast of everything going on in VA. Black knew Bo, a nigga he put on and taught, was running everything, but this muthafucka snitched on him and Lo to save his own ass. They never caught Black, and he was still wanted. He knew Lo got fifteen years, had done three, and was home almost a year and was scrambling. He also heard that his brother Dee was in Charlotte with Chanel, but they had bounced to Atlanta. He knew Chanel was always going to hold Dee down, but what was Dee doin'? Poppa had said something about promotional shows.

* * *

Polite and Black sat out in front of Applebee's on Flatbush in the black-tinted Range Rover, checking everything coming from the mall on Fulton. Making a U-turn in front of Junior's, something caught Black's eye and got his adrenaline running. Black couldn't believe his eyes as the baddest bitch in Brooklyn parked her Lexus truck and walked over and got in a black Tahoe.

A nigga jumped out and hollered at his man, as the woman got in the truck. Black couldn't believe his eyes, it was JB. The one nigga that had his life on hold, the one he always looked over his shoulder to check if he was there. Here he stood four cars away.

"Yo, Polite, get ready. Crucial move."

Polite became alert. He knew one thing about this VA nigga—he was ready and prepared for anything. And once in action, the thought of turning back wasn't an option. "What's the deal?"

Black pulled off slowly, following the Tahoe. He moved through traffic so he could position himself two car lengths behind. JB never even suspected the black Range.

"What you gonna do in all this traffic?"

"Fuck this traffic and fuck these New York niggas." Revenge was already in Black's eyes. He looked at Polite. "I'll meet you in Wilmington tomorrow. Jump over here niggas and use your gadgets." Black pulled back his leather FUBU coat and removed his "nines," put one in each chamber, and jumped out the truck. He walked at a rapid pace as all the other people did on the street and shortened his steps as he reached the driver side of the truck and looked JB in his eyes.

JB's eyes widened and terror covered his face—as did glass and hot bullets. Bullets pierced through the windshield and ripped through not only JB, but also the beautiful passenger that sat beside him holding his hand like lovers out on a Sunday cruise.

People yelled and began scattering. Black disappeared into the crowd and never stopped or looked back until he was able to sit down on the train. His heart was beating at a rapid pace as a feeling of satisfaction filled his entire body. He placed his head in his hands and thanked God for giving him the opportunity to close a bad chapter of his life.

Chapter Two

It was early, and Black had beat the sun up, something that happened often because of his sleeping habits. He looked up at the building that towered over him, the Fort Green Projects. *From Forty Projects in Queens to 142nd St. Uptown, I done stomped all over this muthafuckin' jungle and made my mark.* He stared in the mirror, "VA nigga, what?" he yelled. "Muthafuckas don't know where I come from—Lake Edward, nigga; LE, baby—niggas better recognize."

He took a long, deep stare into the mirror. His eyes were naturally low, and you could hardly see his pupils. His dark skin barely allowed his perfectly trimmed beard to show. The hardness in his face came from many years of playing the streets.

"Aaron Lee Brooks, better known as Black." He stared into the mirror, thinking of a new alias. "Aka Strong." He smiled as he closed the door to the apartment and carried his bag, which contained all his belongings—two pair Timbs, two pair jeans, green cargo pants, four T-shirts, and his three-quarter length field jacket.

He jumped on the Brooklyn-Queens Expressway and headed the hell out of Brooklyn. He'd destroyed bodies and lives during his stay in New York—two in Queens, three Uptown, two in Brooklyn, and one in Wilmington.

The Delaware body was the only body that actually bothered him, because that shit was over a bitch and not business. He lost count of the bodies he left in the seven cities in VA and Richmond.

For every nigga he killed it had just gotten easier. Easier to see the terror in a nigga's eyes, and seconds later, watch the life slowly slip out of his body then be able to stand and say, "That's my work. And for any man or woman that crosses me or try to stand in my way of this dollar, will experience my work." *It shouldn't have to be like that.*

Black traveled down 495S and made his exit, headed toward Hilltop on the west side, one of the projects that was flooded with drugs. The only other projects that came close to as much drug activity was Riverside on the northeast side of Wilmington. There were other projects, but the money wasn't flowing like these two.

Black remembered when he first came, Polite was on the scene making dough, but the respect he was getting was next to none. He had a nice team of money-making young 'uns, but the real money and survival game came from the man with brains, and mad heart. Black brought all that to Polite's organization, and took him and his team to limits they only dreamed about. Now, after all this time, Polite's organization was on point and booming.

They had learned a lot from each other, but Black's stay up North was over. How was he going to tell his man, captain of the team, that he was never going back to New York? Polite still didn't have to say yes, but Black was going to throw it at him. And under no circumstances was he giving up those two bricks that sat in the stash. He was done with the boroughs of New York and this bullshit-ass town they called Wilmington.

Black pulled into the projects. Young lookout niggas let Polite know Black was coming before he reached the house.

Polite was out front when Black pulled up. As always he had on the fly shit, sitting in his wheelchair. He smiled as his comrade parked the whip and jumped out the GS400 Lexus, shining like the sun.

He knew Black was the reason his finances tripled in the last year. Since he brought Black in to run everything under him, money stopped coming up short. Niggas was paying on time and his weight had gotten up tremendously.

Black never played with the workers or even had conversation for them. "Finish your work and be on time with the money" was all he demanded.

"What up, *P*?" Black gave him a pound.

"You know the deal, Black."

"Strong. My name Strong," Black said sternly to let Polite know that changes had been made since he last saw him moving through Brooklyn at a quick pace after murdering that nigga.

Polite had a new respect for Black; he'd seen

Black handle many situations, but what he did the
other night made him realize that Black was one
of those cats you read about in the *F.E.D.S.* magazine or *Don Diva* that was still free and on the
streets.

"A'ight, Strong. What the deal, baby?" Polite
knew niggas changed their name for one reason—
to kill the other name completely—so he never
questioned the change.

Strong stood over the once tall young man. He
remembered when he first got to Queens how
Polite and Curtis would take on any two cats; two
on two for any amount of money.

"Gotta burst on me?" Polite prayed he would
hear something different.

"Let me holla." Strong moved behind Polite
and began pushing him from listening ears. "My
business in New York is done. I gave New York four
years of my life. The streets of New York saved me,
taught me, and brought me back to life, but I've
dreaded every minute."

Polite looked back at him. "Every minute?"

Strong smiled."Not every minute."

"I know damn well. 'Cause we can ask Sandra or
Monique."

"Bitches been good to me, but you know me.

"This what's up—I got peoples in VA waiting on
me; peoples in Carolina. Those credit cards and
checks ain't the only thing poppin' in that tri-city
area down South. Now, I'm not tryin' to stop any
of this flow, I'm sayin', 'Expand.' Right now Rell
and Rico are buyin' twenty kilo each. You come in
and you are buyin' ten. If you buy ten more, all of
your prices go down and everybody makin' more
money. Right now you're slowin' them down."

"Another ten! Whoa, Strong!"

"Lot of work only in the beginnin'. Give me two to three months and I'll be moving ten ki's a week."

"You can't leave me hangin', Strong," Polite said like a sad kid.

"I'm not. You got Li'l Wayne in Brooklyn that's ready to step up; he's put in mad work and it's time. He knows the job.

"I'm gonna get everything set up down the way and I'll be back here. Plus, you got peoples up here while I'm gon' to hold you down . . . without a question."

"Kev and Kev," Polite said.

"Hell yeah, I know Kev is a live wire, but he will listen to you and I know shit won't happen while I'm gone. And Kev, you think all he want to do is play ball, smoke, fuck, but believe me, nigga, he gonna make sure he get that money first. Always."

"One thing, Strong," Polite said with a crooked smile, "you right, but Kev gots to get the fuck up out of here. He cut a kid up last night."

"What?"

"Yeah, over a fuckin' bet."

"That PlayStation shit," Strong said, disgusted.

"Yeah, I'm tryin' to get him back home."

"Queens?"

"Naw, man, our peoples from *Ten-a-key*—Memphis, Tennessee," Polite said, proudly reppin' his home.

"That nigga said that tattoo meant *Making Easy Money Pimping Hoes In Style*."

"Straight pimpin', nigga. You don't know." Polite smiled.

"Well, I'm gettin' ready to make moves. I'll carry

him to VA. I got two of them things in the car. I'm goin' to VA, then to Carolina. He on his own after that."

"So when you plan on seein' me on them things?" Polite asked quickly, not really concerned about the money, but agitated that Strong could only carry Kev so far.

"Two weeks tops; aimin' for one."

"You got two of my things. I'm lettin' you burst and set your own thing up, and you can't do me this one and make sure my cousin get home safe and help us set up shop down there?"

"And what, nigga? Oh! Hell naw. I don't know shit about way down South."

"You ain't know shit about New York, but you played the concrete jungle like it wa'n' shit. I'm goin' down there in a minute; I just need my backbone and my legs down there with me." He smiled at Strong. "And don't forget, nigga, when you left VA somebody looked out for you. I know ain't nobody suppose to know and I didn't ever think I'd have to use it—but don't forget I use to fuck with your cousin Leeta, nigga, and you know pillow talk is a muthafucka. Now go get my cousin from Shana house, then carry yo' ass to VA and get your crown. You never know, you might can use his ass down there. Then I'll meet y'all in Memphis later and finish up business. But for now, he got to get the hell out of here. And since you takin' my shit and bouncin', I don't think I'm asking too much." Polite looked at Strong in his eyes. They both knew the tightness they'd shared—the streets had brought them as close as two niggas could get.

*   *   *

Strong pulled in front of Shana's house. Kev could barely make out the driver as he came out the apartment. As he approached the car cautiously, he checked his waist for security; his four extra pounds that he never left the house without.

Strong saw his actions and rolled down the window so he could make out the image through the tint. Last thing he wanted was to lay this young 'un down over mistaken identity. "Hurry up, shit—pretty muthafucka."

"Shut the hell up, nigga." Kev tried to pull his sagging jeans up and hold his bag. "You know I had to lay this dick down before I left . . . show a bitch how a pimp get down." He closed the door, laughing.

"Bitch cryin' 'cause I'm leavin'. Say she comin' to New York to see me. Bitch, I ain't goin' to New York, I'm carryin' this dick down South. I ain't never comin' back to this little, dirty muthafucka." Kev laughed so hard, he had tears in his eyes.

"Knock that dirt off your shoes, nigga."

"Ain't no dirt on these, fool. These fresh white ones out the muthafuckin' box."

"Can't go wrong with a fresh pair Uptowns. Never go wrong. What's in the bag?"

"Drawers, cosmetics, two ounces of raw, and my 'nine.'" Kev said it like it was nothing. "Oh and two ounces of that good green and hundred of those B's. See what those niggas and ho's know about that Ecstasy.

"I know this phat-ass shit got some secret hole or something."

"No doubt." Strong helped Kev to open the stash. "We out," he said and pulled off, headed toward the Delaware Memorial Bridge. "And roll the fuck up, you already high."

"Goddamn, it's a beautiful day. Sun shinin', skies clear, little chilly, but I'm straight." Kev passed the Wild Rum Backwoods.

"Yo, Shana did your braids?" Strong checked out the design she had freaked in Kev's head.

"Yeah! She nice."

"Don't you got two strikes, son?"

"Yeah! And I was lookin' at number three before I got in this Lex and brought my ass." They both smiled at the convenient escape.

"Got to hold that shit down, kid. You just turned twenty-one and I know you've done some wild shit in your life time and I know you done seen some money, but you ain't seen shit yet, son. And you getting ready to do life over a gee and John Madden." Strong had a frown on his face as if to say, "Are you out your mind?"

"It wa'n' John Madden; it was NBA 2000."

They both began laughing knowing it was a wild move as the 20-inch chrome rims carried the GS400 down 13 South.

"Yo, Black, you right."

"My name Strong. Anybody call me Black know me and my past—that's a major threat, Duke."

"True. True." Kev thought about changing his name. "I ain't no killer, Strong. I caught a felony for beatin' a nigga down. I didn't know he was a diabetic. And the nigga last night, I been knowin' that nigga for years. You wouldn't believe it, but when I heard he died this morning, it fucked with me. Every nigga I've killed keeps poppin' in my head. At night a nigga be 'noid. I mean scared. Nobody knows how I fight with those fuckin' demons. That's why I stay high, stay drunk, stay rollin' off that Ectasy. If I'm not fucked up, I'm ballin'—that, or I'll lose it." Kev stared straight ahead in a daze.

Strong handed the cashier ten dollars for the toll to cross the Chesapeake Bay Bridge.

As Strong came off the Chesapeake Bay Bridge a reality check hit him hard. *These are dangerous streets and my presence need not be known for the moment.*

The bridge ended, and North Hampton Boulevard began. He made a left on Diamond Springs Road, heading toward the notorious Newtown Road. "This is LE, baby. All those apartments right there is Lake Edward West; all those townhouses behind that shopping center. See the hair salon, New York Hair Design, Beads and Bangles, Beauty Supply Store—check out that shit." Strong was taking in the changes.

"Nigga, stop actin' like this shit ain't hood. You got the Chinese spot, check cashin' spot, dollar store, Jamaican restaurant—this shit straight hood." Kev laughed out loud.

Strong made the right on Baker Road. He knew he was home. "Over here on the left, you got Lake Edward too."

"Damn, you basically got a little city of row houses." Kev smiled, realizing the potential that this little city had.

Strong never responded in no way. His mind floated back to his peoples and family. Riding by where Auntie used to live fucked him up.

As he crept past his moms' court, his heart dropped. Moms was holding the door while Auntie and Tony T carried bags in the house. His eyes watered; he knew family was everything and everything he had ever done was for family.

Kev never saw Strong's emotions behind the tinted Cartiers. Strong kept flowing through as he caught eyes focusing in on the new Lex rockin' New Jersey tags. "Young niggas hangin' on the corners not doin' shit; not getting' a goddamn penny."

"Broke as hell. We passed about sixty niggas, only ten look like they workin'."

"Shit's about to change; the bullshit is over. Yo, nigga, there's my cousin Lo. That's my ace, goddamn!" Strong wanted to jump out and hug the nigga and tell him everything was going to be all right. But he had waited four years. *What was a couple more days, if it meant sticking to the plan?* "Lo and Mike Mike." *What the hell were they doing on the corner?*

Poppa had already said Bo shitted on Lo when he came home—no dough, no work, nothing. Just a "fuck you, nigga"—after Lo put him on.

"Yo, them cats starin' real hard."

"Who? Mike Mike and Lo?" Strong smiled, showing his four gold crowns that rimmed out his front teeth.

"This what I'm talkin' 'bout, son."

Strong pulled by the packed basketball court that sat right in the middle of the notorious projects. "Don't get hype now, nigga; it's not playtime, and plus you have to get to Memphis."

"Yeah, but not today and not tomorrow." Kev was going to show Black he needed him right here.

The girls out LE were nice; young girls about sixteen and looking like twenty. Black watched him act like a kid in a toy store.

"These bitches phat as hell, and they ain't wearin' shit. Like they don't know it's fifty degrees out this bitch."

Black wasn't impressed—nine out of ten times either he, Lo, or Dee, had fucked their older sisters, momma, cousin . . . somebody.

"See the cat with the 540 BMW over there with all those gay-ass niggas around him? That's Bo with the bald head and his man, Nat. They runnin' LE right now. That's the same nigga that turned on me and snitched on Lo. I hope that nigga run was good." Strong turned his attention to some other cats. "See those niggas over there with the 4Runner, Jag, Q-45, with all the young ho's over there being grown. Those niggas from Carriage Houses right around the corner; it's not really a project, but you got mad Section 8 out that bitch. So you know how the story goes—momma don't got it, young niggas gon' get it."

"What about them niggas?" Kev asked, plotting on the niggas in his new surroundings.

"As they say, nigga, ride or die. They'll get a call from Strong and ride, or they'll meet Black and die. I don't give a fuck. I'm back with a vengeance, and this is all my money. I got something for all these niggas.

"Let's go get a room and call Poppa."

"Who's Poppa?"

"That's my link, baby. He been eatin' off my plate. Bo goin' through about ninety ounces a week. Poppa only movin' half of that but risin' fast off clientele that Bo was missin'—Damn! That's my little nigga. See dude with the black Cadillac Escalade. Nigga name Javonne. Poppa said he was comin' up, usin' the same style as me. See him by himself, with only bitches around—that's what I taught that nigga. He don't fuck with nobody. Do his own thing . . . in and out of town. True hustler. Poppa say he movin' about a brick a week. One call and he'll be gettin' that brick right here."

Chapter Three

Strong headed to the interstate after showing Kev all the clubs that sat off Newtown Rd: Picasso's, Par 5, and VA's finest, Shadows, where all ballers ball. He headed downtown to the Sheraton. He wanted to run shit as they did in New York. If he could get these slow-ass niggas to respect the game and respect the chain of command, he could put Lake Edward housing on a big-city level and this run should be real sweet. He arrived at the Sheraton and called Poppa.

"Yo, who this?" Poppa yelled over the music.

"Strong."

"Who?"

"Turn the fuckin' music down."

"What the deal, Black, man?" Poppa asked, catching the voice.

"Call the number back to see where I am ... room 412 and bring dat, a'ight."

"One," Poppa said, knowing the number was local. *Was Black home or just a new cell?* He strolled to the caller ID on the cell and found the number and pressed send. "Y'all niggas, shut the fuck up—I can't hear shit," Poppa yelled to four guys standing around his Ford Explorer.

"You don't tell me shit. You from the other side anyway. Carry you' ass back to East Hastings, nigga." Mike-Mike passed the Grey Goose to Lo.

"Tell 'im, Lo."

The four guys were all laughing.

Lo took a swig of the Grey Goose. "That nigga know Buc. I'll burn his ass up quick." Then he hit his "deuce deuce" of Heineken.

"Fuck y'all laughin' at? Who the fuck is you two niggas?" Poppa looked at the two cats hanging around. "Better go on before niggas get spit on—this is fuckin' business." Poppa's face was expressionless.

Two of the guys eased away and began stepping. They knew of Poppa's reputation; the nigga stood six feet, dark-skinned and looked ruff all the time. He wore a gritty look on his face as if he was aggravated at the fact you were looking at him. His hair was cut in a short 'fro, that looked good coming out the barbershop, but it didn't get touched again until the following week. No comb, no grease, just a dry 'fro with a hellified "edge up." His baggy jeans and XXXX white T didn't do much to hide his two-hundred-and-ninety-pound frame. Conversation was minimal, and his patience was shorter than that.

Poppa was Lake Edward born and raised. His peoples had moved twice, trying to get away from the clutches of Lake Edward that kept sending young men to the penitentiary and to an early grave. Plaza and Atlantis Apartments, farther in the beach, were short stays. Not only was he still in the streets, but now he was around niggas he didn't know, and that was beef within itself. Soon they found themselves back on East Hastings. Poppa didn't care—he loved LE; LE respected him. And he was quick to let a nigga know that LE was where he rest.

When he got older he took the moves as a way of meeting new niggas from across town. Poppa would disappear for months, then resurface, go away for a year, then resurface.

It didn't take long for everybody to realize he was trouble. But he just wanted to be like all the legendary hustlers that came from LE: Big Chris, Reese, Cadillac, Black. Everybody dreamed of rising to the status of Black before his team got scooped, or Cadillac, before he started sniffing dope and robbing niggas to find himself laying face down in the gutter in the back of LE on the Norfolk side.

"Hello, hello." The voice brought him back to reality.

"Yes, where is this?"

"Sheraton downtown. Waterside."

Poppa hung up, and a smile came across his face. *This is what I've been waiting four years for. This dough I'm getting is peanuts to what Bo tearing off.*

Bo always slept on Poppa because he knew Poppa didn't know nobody to score weight, and his connect was always straight. Poppa, on the other hand, never killed Bo because of Bo's stability. Bo had learned from the best, one of Black's Lt. So he rode along with Bo and plus he kept himself out of the limelight, and still made a living. But if this was the call that he'd been waiting years for, sorry, nigga, but you gots to go.

"I'm out, niggas," Poppa yelled to Lo and Mike-Mike.

"Drop us off on the other side," Lo said.

"I'm tired of this walkin' shit. I'm gonna get me a Lex with 20's like that shit we saw earlier," Mike-Mike said.

"Fuck that nigga shit. You suckin' his dick like that's your man. I done been through them shits—fuck them niggas' shit."

"You *use to have*, always talkin' that 'use to' shit, and your ass been walkin' since you came home." Poppa and Mike-Mike started laughing.

"Fuck you, son," Lo said.

That let Mike-Mike know he was getting to Lo, so he started up again. "Simple-ass nigga talkin' about when Black come back they gonna do this and that. Always talkin' about what you *use* to have. Now you a broke-ass nigga who drink and stay fucked up like me. That's why you my boy." Mike-Mike hugged on Lo. "But you know Black either dead or locked. He probably locked—that nigga was off the muthafuckin' chain."

"One day, nigga. One day!" Lo said, leaving it alone.

Lo felt bad inside. He was making a couple hundred a week. (Helping Auntie with the rent and taking care of his kids was leaving him "ass out.") Selling what Poppa fronted him was hard because his clientele wasn't what it used to be and he needed real weight to confront the niggas he did know like that. So he stayed scrambling. Nobody knew, but the hopes and dreams that Black would one day appear out the blue was the only thing that kept him looking forward to another day. To find out Black was dead or locked somewhere would have crushed his entire world, and for saying that shit, anybody else might've found themselves stretched the fuck out. But Mike-Mike and Poppa were fam. Close as childhood friends could get.

Poppa knocked on the door to the hotel room. Strong opened the door and signaled for him to come in. Poppa was used to Black getting straight to business and being out. This time was different; he seemed a little more relaxed. Poppa came in and handed Black a bag, and Black passed it to Kev.

"Kev, this is Poppa—my man and definitely part of the fam. A friend of ours." They all laughed as Black imitated the Italians. Even though it was meant as a joke, Kev got the picture.

"Poppa, this is Kev, my little brother." Poppa looked at Kev. He knew Black only had two brothers, Dee and Junie, and Junie was dead. So if he referred to this young 'un as his brother, he was to be accepted, trusted, and not to be fucked with.

They gave each other a pound and sat down.

"So what's the deal, Black? Tell me something good."

"Strong—Black is dead; nigga from the past—call me Strong. If Black show up, it's just like the Grim Reaper poppin' up." Kev laughed while he licked the Backwoods.

"This is what's good, Poppa—I'm here now and it's my time to fuckin' shine. Right now we been movin' a brick here and there, but you got clientele now. How many bricks Bo movin'?"

"About two a week . . . with the help of those Carriage House niggas."

"So after those niggas gone, they'll be lookin' at you for those things. I got to move ten of those things a week; my weights has got to come up. You along with Lo and Kev are gonna lock down LE again, the right fuckin' way."

Kev pulled on the Back and smiled, knowing Black had just included him in his plans to come up and he wasn't going to Memphis no time soon.

Black begin putting things together in his head. A few more contacts and shit would be flowing like talking about it. "I just need y'all to hold down LE . . . because that shit's a gold mine. Everything will be ran out of there."

"It's a lot goin' on out LE," Poppa explained. "Different niggas doin' different shit."

Kev told him, "All that's goin' to change. If it don't come in a blue valve, then it's not sold. We not tryin' to control the city, just get our share."

Poppa listened. *Evidently Black had been talkin' to him about the entire plan.*

"I'll spend the next week settin' up shit, and then it's on. Where niggas fuckin' around at tonight?"

"Shadows," Poppas said. "Real niggas and the fake-ass ones be up in there. But if niggas movin' weight and tryin' to shine, they in that bitch."

"Well, that's the muthafuckin' spot," Kev said. "Somebody gots to get on this head."

"Tomorrow we goin' to sit down and I'll lay

down the plan. So you and Lo come by here to-morrow, and we'll get this shit poppin'. Especially with this nigga, Bo." Strong stared at Poppa.

"Gotta watch that nigga, Black—I mean Strong. He came a long way; he won't be easy to get."

Black looked at Poppa and smiled, showing his gold crowns. He stared at Kev and nodded his head towards Poppa as if he didn't believe what Poppa said.

"When it's time for that nigga to be touched, he'll be touched with no muthafuckin' problem—believe that shit." Kev pulled on the Backwoods and stared at Poppa. *I'll touch your ass too, nigga. Fuck these VA niggas.*

"So the bag straight?" Black asked.

"Forty-six, exact."

"My man, I'll probably be at Shadows tonight. Come through; bring Lo. Yeah, I been meanin' to ask you—seen Carlos?"

"Yeah, man," Poppa said slowly, "Carlos be wildin' out. You don't see him that often because he on paper. Niggas say he sniffin' too."

"Coke?"

"Naw, that 'boy'! Say that diesel got him on a robbin' spree. Last I heard he robbed Tooty, his own fuckin' cousin." Poppa started laughing but tried to hold it in. "He ran up in his own cousin shit, made his girl get butt naked, lay flat, and robbed her."

Strong and Kev started laughing; Kev, because he just heard another wild story, Strong, to keep the hurt from shining through. *Carlos was his boy and he shouldn't be living like that.*

Black knew, outside of the business, many issues had to be addressed. First things first—find out what's going on with Dee; he needed his big brother to hold him down, and he needed Lo on the street close by. Poppa had held him down, but Poppa was not blood.

On top of all that shit, he had two kids that he hadn't seen in four years.

Chapter Four

The last eight months of Angela's life had brought about a drastic change. She'd just had Damien's son (he was murdered seven months ago) and was finding out what it was to struggle.

After getting pregnant and quitting school, her parents cut her off. Now she and her two-month-old baby were living with her cousin in a two-bedroom in Norfolk. Her car needed tires, a tune-up, and gas, and she was down to her last forty dollars.

Thank God her moms bought her baby anything and everything, but their relationship changed. Their conversation was short, with how she fucked up her life usually ended up being the topic. But her moms was right down the street and didn't want Angela leaving him with just anybody, so she made herself accessible.

Angela had just dropped him off and was walking into her apartment. Her cousin April was sitting in the living room drinking with a friend.

April was five feet nine with a medium frame,

had brown skin and an athletic body with small breasts (about a B cup). She wore a short cut that fit her slim face and was sitting with a butch-ass-lookin' bitch, who was wearing Timbs and a sports bra to press her titties down. "What you doin' tonight?" April didn't even give Angela a chance to set her bags down.

"Why you askin'?" Angela asked with an attitude.

"I need a little something on the rent, cuz. It's been two months and I haven't ask for shit. But I know what you doin' and you can give me something."

"Fuck is you talkin' about, April?" Angela didn't appreciate her bringing this shit up in front of company.

Truth was April hated Angela even though they were cousins. Angela had always had better opportunities in life and never took advantage of those easy roads. Even when she was shining in the streets with her ballin' friends, she never showed April love until she had nowhere to turn.

"Word is that you out there shakin' your ass for money. Glad you got your shape back real fast so you can use that money-maker, huh." April sipped on some Henny.

Angela could tell she was fucked up, and her little girl-freak friend seemed even more laid back. Even though April opened her house to her, Angela still thought she was funny and all about money, and just wanted to put enough dough away and get the hell out on her own. Just her and Li'l D.

"Before you say shit, hit this blunt." April held the blunt out for her.

Angela turned from her room and took it.

* * *

Angela had started doing private parties with Monica, but when it came to sex, she hadn't had a man in almost a year. How the fuck she got here, she didn't know. She figured she needed money and Monica was doing it. *So why not?* she thought. And she was getting dough, as she would tell it.

Angela was only doing parties across the water in Hampton and Newport News, to miss the local niggas she went to school with. She had done several parties, but it had been a minute. *How did April know?*

"Girl, I haven't danced in a while."

"You dance?" the other girl asked, like she didn't hear the conversation.

"Not like that."

"This is Shannon," April said. "We've been friends since middle school. She was living in DC, but she back now."

"Nice to meet you." Angela felt relaxed—no, higher than usual—after hitting the blunt. She poured herself some Belvedere.

"Your girl gone, ain't she?" April asked.

"Who? Monica?" Angela had a confused look.

"That bitch doin' more than dancin'. Niggas say she fuckin' for the money now."

Angela took a gulp of the Belvee and looked down. She was hurt. That was her girl, but she had started lacing blunts with crack, then moved to smoking right out the pipe. That was a knife in her heart. "Who said that shit?"

"Bitch, that shit true. She smokin' that shit too. Niggas out the way say she suckin' dick and all that. You better stop fuckin' with her. You ain't had no dick in a year and about to be called a trick."

Shannon smiled and looked at Angela. "It's been that long? So all you do is dance?"

"That's it—just dance. As soon as I get enough to get my own, I'm outta here."

"Carry your ass then." April looked at Angela. "You too fuckin' prissy any goddamn way."

"So you still dance?" Shannon asked again.

Shannon and April had laced the blunt with PCP, and they hit lightly and passed quick. April wanted to get her cousin and passed the blunt back to her.

Angela made the front of the blunt turn bright red and held it—she was taking in way too much.

After gulping down her drink, she began to head to her room. She stood up and the room began spinning. Suddenly she lost her balance, and Shannon was right there to catch her.

"Damn, this shit good. I'm going to get a shower."

Shannon looked at April and threw her hands up as if to ask, "What's up?"

"I'm going to bed." April smiled and walked to her room.

Angela walked to hers and pushed the door. Through a slight opening in the door, Shannon, who sat rolling another blunt, had a clear view of the mirror and stared as Angela removed her clothes and grabbed her robe and made her way to the hall bathroom.

"Hit this right quick!" Shannon told her.

"Shit, I can't stand up now." Angela took the blunt and hit it hard twice before walking to the bathroom.

Shannon sat down and poured herself a drink, waiting patiently until Angela returned. Then she passed the blunt to Angela as if she'd been smoking all the time.

Angela smoked and sipped until she sat nodding off like she was on heroin.

"So what's going on with you, Angela?"

Angela began talking with Shannon.

Shannon knew a little about Angela from what April had told her and kept steering towards her past to try and play on her emotions.

Angela was on a high she had never experienced, and as she began to talk, depression and sadness took over her mind and thoughts. Her eyes watered as she talked with Shannon.

Shannon reached out and hugged her and watched as Angela's robe began to gap and unfold. "Go ahead to bed," Shannon told her; "I'll check you tomorrow."

Angela stood to walk in the room, and Shannon followed, holding her arm to assist her.

"Girl, I'm fucked up." Angela fell across her bed, not moving.

Shannon kept talking to her and nudging her to see if she was awake. After five minutes Shannon knew she was out. She slowly pulled Angela's robe off in the dim lights and began rubbing her. Shannon couldn't believe the perfect figure that was lying beside her had a two-month-old baby. She kept rubbing her hands across Angela's breast, knowing that when her nipples hardened she would respond to what she had in store for her.

Angela felt the hands, but with the dim lights, the laced weed, and the alcohol, her judgment was impaired. Her blurred vision and the close cut of the silhouette brought thoughts of Damien. "Damien," she murmured.

Shannon took Angela's dark nipple into her mouth. Then she took her other nipple between her fingers and, at a snail's pace, massaged them both with her tongue and fingers.

Angela began to let out sighs as she tried to gain control.

Shannon let her hand slide down Angela's stomach and rest on her lower stomach. She unhurriedly took her fingers and massaged Angela's clit. The wetness allowed her long, slender middle finger to slide into Angela's warm, moist vagina. Shannon massaged Angela's spot until her body tightened around her finger. Shannon smiled as her experienced fingers roamed in and out of Angela, and Angela's legs began to open. Shannon eased down and placed herself between Angela's legs. She gradually began rubbing her tongue up and down the inner lips of Angela's vagina, then across her clit. Then she leisurely and lightly sucked, flicking her tongue around.

Angela's moans got louder, and she reached down and grabbed Shannon's head.

Shannon pushed her tongue deep into Angela's tight, hot box. Her lips covered the rest of her hole, and with no air being able to escape, she forced a gush of hot air into her vagina.

Angela's almost lost it when it was done repeatedly.

Shannon reached to the foot of the bed and strapped something across her pelvis as she greedily licked and sucked at Angela's pussy. She eased up and planted a sloppy kiss onto Angela lips before guiding herself between her open, waiting legs.

After cumming several times, Angela's head began to clear slightly. She lay there in Shannon's arms confused. She wanted to say get the fuck out and slap her dike ass, but Shannon's touch felt better than good.

The morning came quickly. When Angela opened her eyes, Shannon was standing over her, looking like that butch bitch she saw the night before when she came through the door.

"How is my girl doing?"

"Fine." Angela answered as if talking wasn't in the plan.

"You did a lot of talking last night. I want you to get your car together and get yourself together. Get some new thongs and bras"—Shannon reached down and got Angela's panties off the floor—"this tacky shit here ain't the fuckin' answer." Shannon tossed the panties on the bed. Then she handed Angela five hundred, kissed her lips, then left.

Angela lay there fucked up and confused, but figured she'd come to a conclusion later; right now she had five hundred dollars.

Two months had passed and for once in a long time, Angela felt like she had peace of mind. Her and Monica were cool again, and that bullshit April was kicking was just that—some bullshit.

Angela didn't agree with anything beyond dancing, but she couldn't say shit because Monica didn't agree with her so-called friendship with Shannon.

Monica had become all business, and her street game was coming together, hooking up with a clique of money-making bitches, whereby all parties and engagements were set up by Queen Bee.

Queen had built a rep. If she put you down with her team, she made sure you got money and demanded that you carry yourself like a lady. That you carried yourself like money. Queen took no shorts, and, whatever a nigga desired, she had a girl for ya.

But Monica always turned heads, and this way of life was no different and it was working. She had a new used SC300 coupe and a one-bedroom condo, just to let bitches know she was handling her own.

Her crazy night-running and still trying to take classes was no joke and had begun to take its toll. Her new party drug had become something to help her cope with life—she had fallen into sniffing an eight-ball a day and not missing a beat.

Angela reminisced about their last conversation.

"So how's little man?"

"He's fine. With my moms and his uncle."

"Your little brother growin' up, huh?"

"Yeah, so what's the deal—is this dancin' shit gettin' you up?" Angela asked, cutting to the chase.

"Hell naw. Just gettin' me by."

"Is these niggas still payin' you well to suck dick and fuck?" The shit Angela had heard was fucking with her.

"Is that bitch payin' you well to eat her pussy?" Monica knew her friend got a raw deal, but so did she. And at this point in their life, neither could really smile or look each other in the eye.

"I don't eat pussy; I can't even touch her. Talk what you know about, dick."

"I don't got time for this, Angela. Sometimes I believe you mad because our lives switched. We still peoples, Angela. And I'm gonna tell you—you need to find a man. Somebody you can chill with. And he'll look out for you and my nephew. Instead of you and that nasty bitch bumpin' pussies. What the fuck you get out of that anyway?—Naw, don't tell me! Fuck it, it's your life."

"I got more respect for myself than to sell my body. What I can't get dancing, I guess I won't get it. Talk your ass off. I even heard you fuckin' with Rome brother, Bo. You done stepped into the big leagues, huh?"

"Every now and then we hook up—that nigga got dough. If I do fuck, niggas come off a gee or better. That's how Queen got us livin'. Broke niggas can't fuck with it; fuck what you heard! Do your dike-ass bitch got it like that?" Monica moved closer to Angela, "'cause I ain't slowin' down for nobody who can't hold me down."

"Later, girl. Stay up." Angela watched her girl shit on her life. Her mind drifted to thoughts of Shannon. She wasn't able to defend her against Monica. *Why?*

Ever since this new relationship, Angela hadn't spent much time with her friends. She ran into

Rome and he was telling her that his brother was kicking it with Monica, but he was in a big hurry to go meet his workers, as he put it, trying to sound like he was the big man.

Rome had escalated up the rankings in the hood. Ski and Quan was moving mad weight, and Fat Joe had started selling powder to some of the employees at the hospital. Rome's little clique was making him plenty money, but everybody new Rome's brother Bo was the man.

Angela got home and Shannon was already there waiting. Once inside she noticed Shannon wasn't her usual self. "What's up with you?"

"Some shit happen in DC earlier in the week and it's not safe to go back. So my sister is moving to Atlanta. I'm going to need to go down there for a while."

"What's 'a while'?" Angela's heart weakened. *Just like a nigga, a bitch come with more shit.*

"My sister knows this guy that bounce at a club down there. He say the club is very exclusive— them ball-playin' niggas and real ATL ballers. You just have to get licensed or some shit and the money is there."

"You want me to go to Atlanta?"

"Why not? Starting over in a new place may be what you need." Shannon knew she could show off this bad, young bitch that she'd turned out.

"When you leavin'?"

"Within a week."

"Shit, I got to talk to my mom, but I'm going. ATL, here I come—fuck with it," Angela said in a loud, hype voice; so many things going through her head.

Angela knew her mother wa'n' going to take the news well. But this was her life, and all the shit she'd been through in VA, she needed a new start.

Even though Shannon was talking about dancing, Angela heard that Atlanta had mad opportunity for black people and that the job market paid well. Dancing was a start. But she felt like she had more in her and it was time to get her shit on.

Angela went to see her moms, and just like she thought, she went through the ceiling.

"You not takin' him anywhere," her mom yelled. "You don't know what the fuck you want to do with your life. You headin' for a life of destruction. And what the hell is in Atlanta?"

"Opportunity and a new start. Mom, you know what I've been through. It's hard here. Maybe I need to get away and get a new start. If it don't work, I can always come back."

Her mom began to cry at the thought of Angela and her new grandbaby so far away.

Ken came from the bedroom. He'd overheard the conversation, especially when their voices got louder. He walked in and hugged her mother. He looked over at Angela. "So is your mind made up?"

"Pretty much."

"If you stay, we'll help you get a place," her moms said through sighs.

"Y'all just don't understand—I need this."

Angela's mom rose up and got her purse. She walked over to Angela. "Look, you do what you think you need to do, but you leave Li'l D here until you get your shit straight."

Angela stood with a lost look on her face, but

she knew it would be much easier with just her and Shannon.

Eventually she agreed. She sighed sounds of relief as she made it back to her car. "Atlanta, here I come," she said, pulling out onto the Boulevard.

Chapter Five

Poppa leaned back in the leather seat on the passenger side as Lo pulled the GS400 in front of Mini Italia in the Newtown Shopping Center. He was in deep thought, wondering what the hell Bo wanted—Bo was still getting his dough. Poppa knew he wasn't going to say shit about the side-money being made, as deep as his pockets were. *And I ain't even started shinin' yet,* Poppa thought. He looked over and saw Bo's LX470.

"Let's go see what this nigga want," Poppa said, even though he knew he was the only one going in to talk with Bo.

Poppa knew Black—no, Strong—was back and what he wanted was going to take power moves—bullets were going to fly, and some would have nobody's names on them.

Mike-Mike and Lo followed Poppa to the entrance of the pizza shop. Poppa gave Rome and Ski a pound as he walked past them to sit in the booth with Bo.

The other four guys stood outside, involved with

their own conversation. "So you comin' up, Lo; that shit phat," Ski said.

"Comin' up, nigga? I been here before; just my time to shine again."

"Hell yeah, just gettin' it back, nigga—better ask a muthafucka." Mike-Mike popped the top on the Heineken and bounced around hype as hell, expressing mad energy.

"Mike-Mike crazy, out this bitch drinkin'," Ski said.

Rome said, "Naw . . . that shit stupid. He be done made the police come over this bitch and fuck with niggas—I ain't got time for that dumb shit."

"Fuck you, nigga. Police ain't fuckin' with you. Who the fuck are you? Oh, you the *brother* of the man." Mike-Mike turned the Heineken up and downed a quarter of the "deuce-deuce."

Lo and Ski laughed.

"Pooh butt-ass nigga," Mike-Mike added.

Rome took offense to the remark but tried to play it off. He thought of punching Mike-Mike, but that would disturb business for his brother. That would make Bo flip. "Who are you, nigga?—a leech. Don't do shit, just hang around." Rome knew Mike-Mike never did shit and Lo always carried him.

"I fuck too, nigga—my girl *and* your girl. Don't forget I really know your girl."

Lo knew he was really getting ready to fuck with Rome, because he did go out with Rome's girl before.

"I know you went out—that's no secret; you was beggin'—but you didn't fuck. Don't lie on your dick, Mike-Mike."

"Never will I lie on my dick, son. I didn't fuck, but I ate her. She let me eat her two times, so next time you eatin' her, ask yourself or ask her, "Am I doin' a better job than the mighty Mike-Mike? She'll know what it mean." Mike-Mike held up his hands then downed the rest of the Heineken.

"You need to get control of your man before somethin' happen to him."

"Ain't nothin' goin' to happen to him. He a'ight—believe that." Lo stared Rome in his eyes, letting him know there was a difference between a hustler and a killer.

Rome played hard, but he knew Lo's credentials. He'd heard horror stories about him and Bo. He didn't want to bump heads with Lo because he knew he wasn't built like that, but he banked on Lo not wanting to bump heads with Bo. That's what made him feel like he had the edge—Bo was still the man and that's how half the niggas in the Beach was eatin', including most of the cats out The Lakes.

Poppa sat across from Bo. Bo, never a bullshit nigga, knew something was up. Poppa had been fuckin' with Bo for over two years, and after that big bust his associates had to go through, it took him almost a year to clear himself and eight months to get back. So he respected him for what he knew and the hustler he was, but Bo had snitched to save himself. Now four years later, the niggas he fucked were back and in a strong way.

"So what the deal, Poppa?"

"Coolin', tryin' to hold it down."

"I'm comin' straight at you—you was doin' a little on the side and I knew it, but you movin' mad shit without me, from what I hear."

"I ain't doin' no more than I been doin'—a brick here and there; I'm just breakin' it down a little more. Couple of young boys on this side of LE got potential. I put them on since all they were doin' were hangin' around the studio rappin', not gettin' shit, but young 'uns turn out to be hungry."

"So you buy that kilo from me, and I'll front you the same; you can front them and more dough is made for us."

"You gettin' yours, Bo. This is me. I'm a'ight."

"Naw, nigga, it ain't a'ight."

Poppa stared at Bo.

Bo stood up.

Poppa stood up.

"The way I see it," Bo said, remembering the tags on the Lex, "you done got comfortable with the New Jersey niggas. You know goddamn well them niggas come to the other side with that shit. My pockets gettin' weaker, and these young niggas doin' it with your help. You rollin' with Lo now, like he your boy. With y'all Jersey connect Lo talked you into, you and him takin' this shit back. Nigga, please . . . Lo can't run this—he ain't Black, and you ain't ready."

With no facial expression Poppa said, "I ain't tryin' to shine; I just want to get mine and eat."

"But it show through your team. I know Tech and Dundee scoring from you. Young boys comin' up and I know it's you, son."

"Them niggas work. I don't know who they fuck with. Wish I could pull them my way." Poppa knew those was his young money-making niggas, but they didn't want to fuck with Bo's snitchin' ass.

Real niggas out the way didn't want no part of him, except to rob him.

"I'm gonna leave it alone for now. Just don't forget who holdin' all this down. Don't forget who brought all these Beach niggas out the fuckin' drought and who put your ass back on your feet."

"You the one, Bo. Much respect." Poppa gave Bo a pound.

"You goin' to go in with me and sponsor this basketball team for the 'Lake Edward Hoop It Up?' Only got a couple months before June."

"I'm straight. Got a squad," Poppa said, exiting the shop.

"Heard that, kid. I'm out. Holla!"

As everybody walked off, Bo and Lo made eye contact and never uttered a word. Rome and Ski jumped in the truck and sped off.

"Fuck that nigga talkin' 'bout?" Lo asked.

"I'll holla." Poppa was in deep thought and didn't want to discuss too much in front of Mike-Mike. He was chill and could be trusted, but when he got to drinking it was no telling what he'd say or do.

Mike-Mike said, "Drop me off Uptown. I'm going to my baby momma house."

"Sit the fuck back, Buc . . . before I tell Poppa how Rome was gettin' ready to fuck you up."

Poppa smiled. "He was gonna fuck him up, Lo?"

They dropped Mike-Mike off out Ingleside and figured to head downtown and catch up with Strong.

"Nigga know we gettin' ready to take over his shit. Talkin' 'bout, he can tell by the way niggas shinin'. Talkin' 'bout you—and I don't know how the fuck he found out Tech and Dundee score from me. Them niggas don't even shine like that."

"Shit, they came to the courts the other day in a new white Tahoe with thirty-day tags, new '99 joint. Black-ass Dundee was laid back, braided up, pushin' the Tahoe like he the shit." Poppa smirked at the thought. "I thought they were putting that money away for a studio. All Tech do is ball, make money, and spit lyrics."

"That's it—write and spit. He gonna make it. Nigga smart, him and those Street Fella niggas, damn!" Lo pulled the CD out of the side-door pouch. "Check this shit. This is Ashy Knuckles, Hannibal, Young Hop, Pop G, and Guttah did the beat. This is the hottest shit I've heard."

They sat listening to five of the hottest niggas to come out of Tidewater and nobody had gotten signed.

"Goddamn, that shit hot," Poppa said.

"Yeah, hot as it comes." Lo turned the music down with the remote. "And niggas don't even fuck with each other no more; niggas actually think they can come up on they own. Young 'uns need some real guidance."

"You right. Some guidance on life and business, not burnin' a nigga ass up. That's part of life too, nigga. That's part of life."

Black and Kev were inside lounging. It was still early in their world. Poppa told Strong about the meeting with Bo. Strong had rushed in and was slowly carving his piece back into the city. Poppa was shaping his team and slowly building his position so, when Bo was gone, his team would be the link to the street. And he had Tech and Dundee. Those niggas had no idea how large they were about to come because every worker would be coming to them, and Poppa would be the man, holding the title, "captain."

"Roll up, Kev," Strong said.

"Already ahead of you," Kev said smiling, with his fronts in. He had been by Strong's side since they hit VA, and he knew he would lock Memphis down the same way. "Check this out—I got some cats comin' up here, two niggas I've known for a while. Friends of mine. They from Bowling Park but been hustlin' down the block forever. Another nigga I know, friend of mine from out Norfolk, he run through Norfolk and Portsmouth. Between the three I figure to move at least six bricks a week. That means it's four bricks for the family, for you and friends of ours. Strong had already made close to two hundred thousand in the three months he'd been back. Now it was time to really get shit poppin'.

"Poppa, your price will be twenty-one thousand a brick. I'm sayin' it now, so when I start talkin' amongst friends you know. Understand!"

Poppa knew the regular street price was twenty-four. He figured he'd sell his halves for twelve thousand, and quarters for sixty-five hundred. Take another brick and break it down. *Goddamn*, Poppa thought, *I'll see four to five off at least two bricks a week.* He knew Lo was going to move the other two. "We gonna set up LE like a fortress. Fiends from everywhere welcome. There's four entrances to LE. We'll have an apartment and row house, entering off Newtown Road, and two young 'uns keepin' watch. Let cats know every time po-po come in. Another joint on Baker Road so you can work and see po-po enter at the light. Get another joint in front of 7-Eleven in Brandywine and Wesleyan and a row house on Blackpoole with the garage. Put two young 'uns out there on the corner of Baker and the Drive. The fourth and last is the easiest and the biggest outlet in the back of LE at the rail that separate Norfolk and the Beach. Gots to have a spot back there on West Hastings. We'll spend about eight thousand a month on cribs, but that ain't shit. Y'all will give the niggas titles and they will all play their position. Everybody gonna eat and eat well; this gon' be a strong and safe work environment."

"So how you plan on gettin' these cribs?" Poppa asked.

"Buy the row houses and rent the apartments. All that's covered. Y'all will have the keys in a couple weeks."

Lo knew what all that meant. Black talked all that business shit, but he knew Black was about putting that raw on the streets and ballin'. Only one nigga handles his business and money, Dee.

A knock came at the door. Lo jumped and put his hand in his waist. Kev jumped and put his hand behind his back. "Calm down; it probably them cats I spoke on."

Strong opened the door, and two dudes walked inside.

"What up, my nigga?" The guy came through the door, giving niggas pounds, then grabbed Strong, showin' love.

"What up, Black?" Mont smiled. It was good to see a nigga that had been hustlin' as long as he was and still shining like he on top.

"They call me Strong now, Mont," Black said sternly.

"A'ight. I'll call you goddamn Saddam, long as the numbers right."

Everybody laughed.

"This my brother Grip."

Grip gave Black a pound and threw his head up at the other niggas.

Mont and Grip was going to hold down the NE side of VA Beach. That left the SW side that connected to Chesapeake and NW side that connected to Norfolk for Poppa, Lo, and Kev to hold down.

"When we hook up, this is a taste of what y'all will be fuckin' wit." Strong threw a bag on the table.

Mont picked it up, put some on his fingernail, and touched his tongue. He knew his powder. When most niggas was hustlin' "hard" like his brother, his clientele was white folks. Mont was a thug to no end. No secret about where he come from—gold in his front, loud when he talk, almost intimidating because of his 5' 11", 280-pound frame, looking like he ate weights. He started lifting when he first started getting locked up. He never stopped getting in and out.

His brother Grip was slightly taller, slightly smaller, but cut as if he ate weights also. He wore house shoes and white T, while Mont rocked all that designer gear.

Mont handed him the bag.

Grip took his nail and scooped some. "What this shit stand?"

"Maybe two. I suggest one," Strong said.

Grip sniffed it and lifted his head. Then he stuck out his chest and shook his head. "A one, nigga; be real." Grip stared at Black.

"I don't care if you put a six on that shit, long as you give me twenty-three thousand, five hundred a brick—five hundred for your smart-ass mouth."

"Come on, man," Grip said smiling; "you can do better than that fuck."

Kev told him, "Fuck what, nigga? This ain't no bargainin' table."

"I just made it one, muthafucka."

"Twenty-three thousand, five hundred, muthafucka. Done!"

"Twenty-three thousand, five hundred, and it will stand two, guaranteed." Strong tried to gain control of the situation. He was depending on these niggas' dough. They were going to buy three bricks a week, seventy gees a week like clockwork. Niggas wa'n' livin' like that these days.

Another knock came to the door, Strong peeped through the peephole and opened the door.

In walked two cats. One was a young boy, and the other looked about Black's age. Young boy was wearing a Rocawear jean suit with butter Timbs. To set it off, he rocked a long, white gold necklace and bracelet. The other cat was a husky nigga with a 'fro, wearin' Levi's, Polo shirt, white Reebok Classics, no jewels, and when he spoke he showed two gold fangs.

Strong turned to everybody and said, "This my nigga, Speed."

Poppa's head snapped in his direction as did Lo's; they both had heard that name before. This nigga was a true street legend, and the treacherous shit he'd done spread throughout Tidewater.

"What the deal, Mont?" Speed gave him a pound.

"Not a thing. Same old shit. When you start fuckin' with this shit here? I thought you only fuck with 'boy' (heroin)?

"This shit is in demand too—I fuck with the money. You ain't tryin' to share, nigga. Make a nigga come and take y'all block." Speed smiled a wicked smile towards Mont and Grip. They knew he was serious, but they smirked it off.

Speed turned towards Black. "So what the fuck you got, Black?"

"Strong. They call me Strong now, Speed." Black was firm, to let him know he wasn't joking.

"I don't know Strong; I know Black and that's who I supposed to be meeting. Now go get him."

"These joints twenty-three, five apiece. This is it." Black handed him the packet.

Speed handed it to the young boy. He took a twenty out and did a one&one then shook his head, looking in Speed's direction. "Thorough, son. Whoooo!!"

"How many? Three?"

"Next week."

"Yeah!" Black was hoping Speed got down. Lot of cats didn't fuck with him because they were scared. He had a hell of a reputation and was somebody you didn't want to go against.

Black stared into his eyes as they negotiated. Speed had the upper hand because he knew he could flip the whole bird and get quick money.

Heroin was his thing, but he had folks, and he loved the hustle, the grind, the streets, and doing dirt was in him. That's why Black was trying to bring him in. He knew in no time he could get Speed buying four and five bricks. He had the money and he knew the people.

Black knew he was a dangerous nigga who had mad bodies and never got locked. What Speed didn't know was that Black's count was running neck and neck, and one more would make him no difference.

Speed agreed.

After burning a couple Backs and pouring some Henny, niggas broke out. Poppa, Lo, Black, and Kev still remained in the room.

"A'ight, Poppa, Lo, y'all know Bo plannin' to get y'all. If he don't, it would really surprise me, so let's hit him. Time to handle this shit."

"If you don't get Rome too," Poppa said, "he gonna come back."

"No, I got plans for Rome first. Then his girl. Then Bo will fall. Feel me, Lo?"

"No doubt, fam. Please, let's do this."

"Look, if I say, bring me a nigga, however you have to do it, bring me the nigga alive and bring him to Balview, out Ocean View. It's a house that sit up on a hill. Got a basement and all. Eight thirty-two is the house number—don't forget . . . because I need Rome soon as possible. One other thing, Lo—call Dee and find out where he at. We out of here tomorrow. I need my brother."

Lo knew already. He knew Dee was going to lose his mind, just like he did when Black and Poppa came up in the poolroom. That time, he thought he'd seen a ghost, until he rubbed his eyes, focused in, and realized it was for real. And when Black handed him the keys to the Lex, he knew his cousin was back and this was not a dream.

Mike-Mike didn't have shit to say that night. All he knew was that his man was back on top—new whip, new gear, and a different hotel every night. After four years, the good life had made its way back around.

Strong, Lo and Kev broke out the next day, headed up 58 to 85S. Six hours later, they pulled in front of a cute ranch-style home in the city of Charlotte, NC. Strong hadn't seen Dee in four years, and his stomach was sick from excitement. Once Dee was by his side, he could find peace of mind on some aspects of the business.

He saw the Mazda Millennium in the driveway. They parked and knocked on the door.

"Who is it?" the voice asked. She pressed her eye to the peephole. "Black," she yelled, trying to get the door open. She couldn't believe her eyes. She stood there, her eyes wide and her mouth open.

"How you, Chantel?" Black asked.

"Fine." She gave him a big hug. She had nothing but love for this man. She reached over and hugged Lo, who she'd only seen once since he'd been home.

She had love for Black, but she knew from his attire and the tinted black S500 with thirty-day tags that he was back and getting money.

"Dee not even here. He's in Atlanta handlin' business. He's down there more than he's here."

"What he doin'?" Lo asked.

"Promotin' shows. Bringing artists to Atlanta. Not doin' bad either. He just catch attitude when niggas try and shine and act like they the shit. He say he hate caterin' to these fake-ass niggas tryin' to play gangsta." She laughed.

"Why don't he do shows here in Charlotte? They say the money here since y'all got the pro teams and shit. Ain't this where all the money at?" Lo asked.

"Dee don't like it here either—he say Charlotte ain't shit, but a good place to live when a nigga retire."

"That's Dee," Strong told her. "Got his own way he see shit."

"He's a spoiled-ass nigga with a bad attitude. He just want shit his way and he ain't gonna do shit he don't want to."

"I don't know. I think some of that's changed. The way he struggled these last couple of years, he will do what he don't want to." She made it seem like Dee was getting soft. Black didn't like the comment but realized that Chantel had the right to say anything she wanted.

She'd been through hell with Dee. One time he got fucked up with another bitch and the girl died, and everyone looked at Dee as if it was his fault, even though he was left fighting for his life. Chantel had taken a leave of absence from her job in Charlotte and came to Virginia to take care of this nigga, then took him to Charlotte when she was no longer able to stay, but continued to nurse him back to health.

"No, he don't have to do shit he don't want to and he will be all right." Strong didn't give a fuck how she took it. "You got a number to reach him?"

"Yeah, 770-671-****. And if you miss him, Ken-Ken can reach him; his number is 404-323-****."

"Ken-Ken from Kappatal Kuts?" Black said to himself out loud.

Lo said, "That's the only Ken-Ken I know that he would fuck with."

Chantel looked on as they all climbed in the Benz and drove off. *Black still that cool, black-ass, money-chasin' nigga.* She knew her life was about to change. Why was her stomach turning? Why did she feel uneasy? Black was home. Wasn't that good?

"This suppose to be the shit," Lo said as 85S changed from a two-lane highway to a six-lane.

"ATL, dirty muthafuckin' South," Kev yelled. "This where niggas from Memphis come and ball."

They searched the radio until the banging sounds of Outkast came pouring through. Black picked up the cell and pressed 1—he had already programmed Dee's number in his phone.

"Who is this?" Dee answered.

"What up, man? Where you at?" Black asked, as if they'd talked earlier.

Dee knew the voice, but this couldn't be—his brother was gone, locked up, like so many people said. Others said and wished he was somewhere dead, but Dee hoped and prayed that neither was true. His hopes and what seemed like a fuckin' dream sat in the back of his head. His life had been fucked up for the last couple years. He was bowin' down and fuckin' with nothin'-ass niggas, compared to the niggas he'd fucked with in the past. He fell to nothing, fuckin' with bitches and really truly depending on them. Then these niggas he was getting money with was fuckin' him and lookin' down on him as if he was some needy, beg-gin'-ass nigga. But Dee had no choice—it was ei-ther get down or drown. Many days he wished God would allow him to never wake up. He prayed for it, but it never happened. And by the grace of God, he was still here for his brother's return.

"Oh my God. Yo, son—what the fuck?" Dee yelled, the eagerness bringing tears to his eyes. He never thought he'd hear this voice again. "Where you at? VA?"

"Naw, Duke, I'm tryin' to find you. Me and Lo on 85 South, headin' into Atlanta."

"Hell yeah!" The anticipation made his stomach turn. Dee tried to give directions, but the words came out scrambled. "Look, stay on 85 South and take 285 towards Decatur and Stone Mountain. Then take I-20 towards the DEC and get off on Candler. Make a left and then you'll see KFC on the right. Pull in there. Hurry up, son." Dee yelled like an excited child.

"One." Black smiled and looked over at Lo, laid back, sipping on the pint of Hennessy he got be-fore leaving Charlotte.

They pulled in the KFC parking lot, and Black instantly noticed the '94 740il sitting in the park-ing lot, looking run-down and dirty, with a dent in the driver side door. "I thought I told him to sell that, Lo?" Black said, thinking out loud.

"You did. He hard-headed, always want to do what the fuck he want to do," Kev said, repeating what he'd heard earlier.

They all laughed as they got out the car.

Dee climbed out on the other side of the BMW.

"I'm tired of this shit." He planted his feet on the ground. "Fuck niggahs hit my shit and kept goin'."

"Hit my shit and kept goin'," Black said as they embraced. "Told you to sell that shit."

"I needed something to drive."

"Yeah, it could of came back on you. Gotta listen sometimes, man," Black whispered as they hugged, so it could only be heard by him.

"So what up, nigga?" Dee punched Lo.

"You know the deal, cuzzo." Lo and Dee embraced.

"You back on yet, nigga?" Dee asked.

"Like you wouldn't believe, fam. Couple more steps and we'll really be back."

"Who dis nigga? Gotta be fam, if he rollin' with the clique." Dee looked at Kev.

"Kev, man." They gave each other a pound.

"So welcome to the ATL home of Jermaine Dupri. This shit is off the hook, Black."

"His name Strong now," Lo told Dee.

Dee laughed. "Strong, Black, whatever. Nobody don't know you down here."

"Is that about to change? Is the ATL ready for Strong . . . because I know goddamn well they ain't ready for this VA-bred, LE-raised, muthafuckin' Black." Everybody started to do the LE yell. Even Kev, who was loving VA about right now.

"So what you got goin' on here?" Strong asked.

"Promotional shit. 3E Entertainment—that's the company name. Doin' this shit, the object is to get in with the local radio personalities and you in there. This deejay here is Frank Ski. He runs the city. If he say it's bond, it's bond. His word is law like the Buda Brothers.

"Then they got this girl, Mama Chula, who's

just like the girl Chris Caliente on 102.9. If they deejay the party, it's packed because of their name and reputation. These clubs here hold more people, and if you do a show you got five million niggas to promote to. How can you lose?"

"A'ight, I hear you. Now what would it cost to bring one of those rap niggas out?"

"Yo," Kev said, "we can't talk about this somewhere else? This shit don't look all that hot; let's get the fuck out of this parkin' lot."

"For real. I don't even know where the fuck I'm at," Lo added.

"Shit, I'm ready to put something in the wind and start rollin'," Kev said.

"Fuck you know about rollin', nigga?" Dee asked.

"Roll with the best, nigga." Kev pulled a small bag containing several Ecstasy pills.

"What kind you workin' with? Let me see one."

Kev handed Dee the bag.

"Aol, D & G, 007, tweety birds. I see, son, you got plenty. Let me see what these D & G feel like." Dee popped one and handed the bag back.

Kev reached in the bag and popped one before putting them back in his pocket. "Yo, kid, that's twenty."

"A'ight, I got you," Dee said. "Roll with me and twist one up."

They climbed in the car, headed north on Candler Road. By the time they reached South DeKalb Mall the trees was in the air and Fifty was blasting through the speakers on a Clue mix-tape.

"Thought you would have it on one of these stations playin' that Down-South bullshit."

"It's a'ight sometimes, but some of that shit is a

headbanger. I got a six-disc changer—Jiggah, Mr. Cheeks, Mobb Deep, Foxy, Jaheim and Clue, son." Dee pulled on the Backwoods. He turned into an apartment complex much larger than the one in VA, but not bigger than The Lakes (Lake Edward).

Dee jumped after Kev, while Strong and Lo found a spot. They followed Dee to the second floor, where they went inside a spacious, two-bedroom apartment and sat down. When Strong and Lo saw Dee put his key in the door, they knew this was his shit.

"Roll up, somebody," Dee said, going into the kitchen.

Lo had already grabbed the remote and turned on the TV and started fuckin' with the stereo.

The bedroom door opened, and out walked a shorty in sweats, bra, and wife-beater. "Hello," the dark-skinned girl with shoulder-length hair said. She walked to the kitchen.

They all looked in her direction in time to see her extremely phat ass jiggle with every step through the sweats. She hugged Dee and turned around with her arm around his waist.

"This is Tricia. Tricia, this is Kev, Lo, and Black—I mean Strong."

Her eyes widened. "Your brother? It's like I know you, Black. Nice to finally meet you. You too, Lo." She turned to Dee and placed both her hands on his stomach. "I'm goin' to take Krystal to my mother's; I'll be back about nine." She kissed him and walked into the other bedroom.

Moments later she returned with a little girl. "Krystal, that's Uncle Strong, Lo, and Kev," Dee said. "That's my muthafuckin' family and yours too."

The three-year-old just looked.

Strong looked at the cute little girl and thought of his own. He also noticed the look in Tricia's eyes when Dee spoke or hugged her. *What was going on here?*

Dee locked the door when she left. "Shorty a'ight." He looked at Strong.

"We can see that. She got peoples and I mean peoples that look like her, phat as hell just like that? Goddamn!" Lo said.

"He ain't lyin'," Kev said, laughing on the low. "And that shit startin' to kick in too."

"That's how they come in the ATL?" Lo finished off his Hennessy. "We got to go to the liquor store before it close; it's almost nine."

"You ain't in VA, nigga. These liquor stores don't close early like that."

"Where Tricia from?" Strong asked. "I know she from Up Top."

"Jersey, son."

"I know. I been up there with that shit for four years; I caught the accent."

"Damn, let me call her and tell her to bring some Henny and Alizé so we can sip on some thug passion. She'll drink that too."

"Me too," Lo said. "That's my shit."

"Bitch drink. You don't mix shit with Hennessy, bitch-ass niggas." Kev laughed. "Thought you hung with troopin'-ass niggas, Strong?"

"Tell 'em, Kev. Fuckin' up the Henny—I don't know them muthafuckas."

Tricia came in about ten. The time had flown by as they sat around catching up on everything and everybody. Tricia decided to call it a night. She knew the boys had to catch up on a lot of things that she wasn't entitled to hear.

Dee excused himself. He went in the room to shower, but Tricia had other plans.

"I need some help going to sleep," she said walking into the shower.

They hugged, kissed, washed each other, and dried off. Dee laid her back and raised her legs. He'd been fuckin' with Tricia for three and a half years. He didn't only know how to make her feel good, but he knew how to make her cum.

And tonight she came quickly. She was out before he could clean up, throw on the Polo jeans, new white T-shirt and Timbs, and squirt on some Black Jean Versace cologne.

"Let's roll. I know y'all niggas ain't tired. Atlanta don't shut down at two on Thursdays. Let's go finish talkin' business, then we'll catch dessert."

They all jumped in the 500 with Dee driving. He adjusted the seat and was admiring the wood grain. *Goddamn! This is a fuckin' car.*

They jumped on 20 East, headed back into Atlanta, to 285 North to GA400. He kept the Benz floating for about twenty minutes, which only felt like ten by the time they reached Exit 5, heading into Sandy Springs.

Dee turned into some townhouse type apartments. "Come on." Dee opened the door. The condo had three bedrooms. Dee closed the room doors and walked into the kitchen. Off of the kitchen was an office. "This is my office, son. This is where I put my deals together." Dee stopped in his tracks, looked at Kev and whispered, "Damn! I feel good as shit."

"Nigga, I'm over here about to jack my dick if I

don't get around some ass," Kev said. "Can we make some money down here, kid?"

"No doubt. I know mad bitches that get down. Next trip down, everybody rollin'," Dee said. "Get shit rollin'."

"Shut the hell up, nigga, talkin' yo' ass off," Lo said.

"Well let me finish talkin' about this business shit," Dee said, directing his conversation to Strong.

"So how you makin' money right now? Who financin' this shit? How much you gettin'?" Strong asked all at once.

"I'm gettin' like twenty percent of the profits, usually around five to six thousand. Niggas Ken-Ken know, VA cats, down here doin' their thing."

"Can I smoke in here?" Kev lit the Backwoods.

"Yeah, but go in the room on the left. She don't like smokin' in her shit. She don't like it around her daughter; plus, she a substance-abuse counselor."

"She need to come out here and go to work," Lo said. We all started laughing and walked in the room.

"This my room."

The room contained a couch, a chair, TV/VCR, and a smokeless ashtray. Lo and Kev stayed, and Strong and Dee walked back to the office.

Black saw that Dee had a computer, scanner, printer, and fax, all the necessities to run a business. "So this is all the promotional shit? You in with the radio peoples?"

"And I'm makin' all the connects and gettin' invites to the big parties. Ball players, rap niggas, their managers—I go straight to the source. I have special guests show up at parties. I make niggas thirty gees, and I walk away with five."

"That's why I asked how you was livin'? Five gees every couple months, girl in Charlotte, bitch in Decatur . . . Who shit is this? And where the fuck we at?"

"Vianna, and we in North Atlanta."

"You got three bitches, the car look like shit, but it's still rollin', yo' gear half-decent—not off five gees every couple months."

"There's a kid down here from VA. He live on the West End. He had niggas comin' down, makin' company checks off big corporations, and even printin' credit cards by the same big company. We would get bitches to deposit them, hit them off, and pick up some change. Dude sister work for Bank of America. She get him credit card numbers and his man make up the credit cards, Visa. Sign it and they aren't suppose to ask for ID, but you know how that goes. That's why I try and get my shit in a bitch name—them ho's get away with murder. Buy today, return tomorrow. Shit ain't steady, but nigga got to do whatever.

"I was fucked up, son. Chantel gave me money to get down here. Vianna gave me dough earlier to take care of some shit. Gots to give that shit back Saturday.

"I got a show tomorrow downtown, 201 Courtland. Local cat you never heard of, but he went gold down here. Cat live in Florida now. Special guest Big Boi from Outkast. Shit will be pack. Thirty thousand will be made."

"It's some money down here . . . street money?"

Strong asked. "Because VA is locked and I'm gonna come through Carolina and then Memphis."

"Memphis?"

"I'll explain when we go. Right now I need you to come to VA and set up everything, work houses, stash house, company shit. Do your thing tomorrow for those niggas, and we out early Saturday."

Dee didn't know exactly how established Black had gotten, but after Black laid his entire plan down, Dee saw the light.

"Black, fuck Atlanta. This is a place for livin'. Do dirt in VA, SC, NC, and even Tennessee. Let me do my thang here, and we'll take this promo shit to another level. It's a lot of clean money here, and to be a millionaire in ATL is a man's muthafuckin' dream. Let's make it happen, son."

"Well, tomorrow's show is the last show you will do with niggas outside the family. From now on we'll finance our own shit. If thirty thousand come in this bitch, it's ours—fuck them niggas. So next time a show is done, it's being brought to you by Triple Strong Entertainment."

Dee thought about his brothers—Junie, Dee, and Aaron, three strong cats. They gave each other a pound.

"Tomorrow's a new day, Dee. Beginning of a new life." Strong smiled at Dee. "Last run was all right, but this time we going to shine amongst the stars, my nigga."

"Amongst the real stars. Believe that." Dee smiled.

"Feel that 'X'?" Strong asked.

"Hell yeah. I need some trees." Dee went to the room with Lo and Kev. "Pass it, nigga."

Kev was laid-back, fucked up. Lo was still sipping on the fifth of Henny and had just tooted up damn near a gram.

"Don't get dead now; we out in a minute." Dee pulled on the Backwoods, passed it to Strong and made his way to the other room.

"What up, baby?" He jumped on top of Vianna.

"Stop. I'm tired. You know I can't go back to sleep when you wake me up."

"I don't give a fuck," was Dee's response as he ran his hand from her arm to her leg and to her ass and gently massaged it.

"I said no, Dee."

He pulled the covers back and slapped her on her ass. "Come meet my peoples. Throw something on."

"Meet who? And I know you aren't smokin' in my den."

Dee was Vianna's man for three years. When she first met him, he treated her like a queen. She was from a well-to-do family of six, and he was a street nigga from VA, running from a past that took her over a year to find out about. He was hard and harsh at times, but when he loved, every moment was like a fantasy slowly being played out.

He got his money in the streets and swore he was never getting a job, and on top of that he stayed high—two things she said would never be in her life. Yet this nigga had a key to her house and car. Dee ran the streets a lot, and it did leave her lonely. If it wasn't for her girlfriend, she would've lost her mind a long time ago.

* * *

"I'm smokin' in the room. My day been goin' good; don't fuck it up with all that bullshit, god-damn!"

Vianna sat up in the bed, her eyes watering as she spoke. "I was just sayin' I don't like no street people comin' here smokin' and—"

"Look, love, have I ever brought anybody to your house since I met you in the three years I've been fuckin' with you?"

"No." She wiped her face.

"If I smoke, don't I go in the room?"

"Not all the time." She stared into his eyes.

"Lately I have, but look my brother and cousin out there."

"Black and Lo?"

"Yeah. Slip something on." Dee stared at her golden brown legs and small, manicured feet sticking out of the purple silk shorts with matching top. He grabbed her by the back of her long, black, curly, wet hair, pulled her head back, and kissed her gently on her little lips. "Hurry the hell up." Then he poked her and said, "Brush your teeth—your breath fuckin' me up," before he returned to his peoples.

They all walked to the den. "What up, Kev?" Dee asked.

"Here, nigga." Kev passed him another X pill.

They turned when they saw the beautiful figure appear. She had brushed her hair back in a pony-tail.

"What up, baby? This Black, Lo, and Kev; fellas, this is Vianna."

"How you all doin'?" She opened the refrigera-tor. "Would y'all like anything?"

"Naw, we all straight," Strong told her.

Then Lo said, "Shit, got any turkey sausage or something?"

"Hold tight. We goin' by Krystal's on the way out." Dee picked up the keys.

Kev looked at Strong. *Damn, that bitch fine. Hope she got some peoples.*

"So where you from, Selena?" Lo asked.

We all smirked, thinking this nigga stupid, calling her the girl from the movie.

"I'm from Texas, but I've been in Atlanta for a long time."

Kev asked, "So what, you Mexican?"

"Mexican and black, baby."

"I thought your ass was Filipino," Lo joked.

We laughed, and she had a look of curiosity on her face.

"If you were in New York people might think you Puerto Rican," Strong explained. "In VA we grew up with Filipinos, not Mexicans."

Vianna stepped in front of Dee. "You comin' back tonight?"

"It's up in the air. Showin' these niggas the ATL."

"Call me." She kissed Dee. "I'm gonna say goodnight. Hopefully, I'll see you all tomorrow or today. Nice to meet you, Kev, Lo, and I'm happy you're back with your brother, Black." She reached out and grasped Black's hand. She knew the deal, this was the brother of the man she loved.

Vianna had faith in Dee, but she'd heard enough "if Black was here" stories every time his back was against the wall. She walked into the room, fell into deep thoughts, then drifted to sleep.

* * *

"Spark up," Dee said.

Kev lit the Backwoods and coasted onto 85S. After riding for about ten minutes, they took an exit and went past the bus station.

"Where we goin', fam?" Lo asked.

"Can't you see, fool?"

Everybody hyped up when they saw the bright lights that read MAGIC CITY.

Lo, in ignorant form and fucked up, sipped on the Henny. "This shit packed. I hope we ain't have to walk a country mile or GA mile—whichever one longer."

Black, nice from the Henny and weed, was nowhere near fucked up, and Dee and Kev just felt real good in the car, talking their ass off.

Dee pulled up in front, parking the car in VIP. Security walked up. "What up, Dee?"

Dee jumped out and put a fifty in his hand. "Put my name on the list for tomorrow; other niggas got that baby." Dee walked away. They knew him from promoting the shows, but balling and handing out fifties, it was like WHO DAT NIGGA!?????

Dee knew he wouldn't be there long. Strip clubs wasn't Black's thing. One thing Black didn't know was these bitches got naked. There was forty naked bitches walking around, titties and ass everywhere, different shapes and sizes, and they carried themselves like ladies with a sense of self-worth, even though butt-ass naked.

Kev had two beautiful-ass, naked bitches giving him a dance fit for a king. In an hour he'd spent two hundred; Lo, about eighty. Dee had given two girls twenty dollars apiece and spent his time talking, hollering at two girls he knew, on some business shit.

Strong had given two shorties fifty apiece. They'd talked and danced for him the entire time without hesitation. When they were leaving, they broke their neck to give him their numbers. Dee knew then that Strong would be coming back.

Lo asked Kev, "Get any numbers?"

"Hell naw. I gave them bitches mine; they gonna call me later."

"Them hoes ain't callin' you, fool. They got your money to carry to the mall. Bitches gonna be in Lennox tomorrow with your dough." Dee laughed along with Lo and Strong.

"Them hoes gonna find a way and call my long-distance number; I'm from Memphis, nigga—I was born a pimp." Kev got in the Benz.

They pulled off towards Peachtree.

Dee leaned over to Strong. "How we livin', son?"

"Real good, and my plans is for us to be millionaires in this fuckin' game, son—within six months."

"Get a room down here?"

"Get a *suite* down here, nigga."

Dee and Strong were sitting in the room talking when the phone rang. It was about 4 a.m. Lo was on the couch 'sleep, and Kev was sprawled across the bed.

Lo jumped up and handed Dee the phone. "Yo, Dee, tell them hoes where we at."

Half an hour later, four of the baddest young

women walked in. Two was sniffing with Lo, and two was smoking with Dee and Strong. Kev had invited them over and they couldn't wake him up. He was out.

Chapter Six

Poppa turned on to Lake Edward Dr*ive*. *I hope they don't have no roadblocks out here today, checking shit. Thank God.* He turned on E. Hastings and stopped about fifty yards from where niggas was making their dough.

He took the paper bag that contained twelve grand. "It's straight, right?" He looked over at Dundee.

"No doubt, baby." Dundee, most of the time mistaken for having a look as if he was runnin' game, spoke in his low, cool voice. "This shit is gone, man; we need more." Dundee said it like he was complaining.

"In just a second, you'll have all you need, then we'll see what the fuck you gon' do."

"You already know I'm ready, son, or you wouldn't be fuckin' with me." Dundee smiled, gave Poppa a pound, and jumped back in the truck with Tech who was already on E. Hastings.

Tech looked at the guys that crowded the corner. "Look at all these niggas, son. I gather it's about thirty niggas out here, and three makin' money—need to clear this shit out."

"Let a couple bodies drop and we'll see the difference in the morning." Dundee palmed the gun that sat in his waist, a reflex action that came with the talk of murder. "But you drop a nigga who the shit, think he bad, and got mouth. Don't kill Pee-wee—he gettin' it out here—or Scotty—he keeps Pee-wee under control and keep his mind on money."

"And that nigga Rome serve both of those niggas," Tech said. "So it's only one way to get them to come our way—ask 'em."

They both started laughing as they drove off in the white Tahoe and threw up peace signs at the young cats on the corner hanging out. Some of the young boys hollered they name.

The rundown row houses, dirty sidewalks and parked cars made the road seem real narrow for two cars. As Tech and Dundee approached Lake Edward Drive, Rome, Ski, and Fat Joe were turning on E. Hastings in Rome's new Ford Expedition. Rome's eyes caught Tech's; Ski's eyes caught Dundee's.

Dundee began quoting:

"Come with me, Hail Mary
Nigga, Run quick see, What do we have here
Now, do you wanna ride or die?"

"Hold tight," Tech yelled. He tried to grab Dundee, but it was too late. He was already halfway out the truck. Tech then slid his hand under the armrest and gripped the chrome .45.

Rome slammed the truck in park and, in one

swift motion, opened the door, and pulled his nine. He began shooting, shattering the Tahoe's front windshield.

Dundee came from the right side of the truck and shot Rome in the shoulder. Rome's gun fell.

Ski had positioned himself out the passenger side window and ended up catching two from Dundee, the bullets ripping through his head and neck.

Rome, meanwhile, had fallen on the truck, and two more shots from Dundee's gun left him lying on the cold pavement.

Dundee looked down at Rome, never bothering to pay attention to the LX470 that was behind the big Expedition. He felt the bullet shoot through his arm as Bo let off shots from the two black nines he held tightly, one in each hand. One gun fired shots through the windshield of the Tahoe, the other in the direction Dundee ran, until he disappeared into the back alley.

Bo ran up to his brother. Blood covered his abdomen, thigh, and shoulder, but his eyes were still open. "Come on, baby. Please hold on."

Fat Joe jumped out the back. He'd been down on the floor from the time he saw Dundee. He looked at Rome on the ground gasping for air, then over at Tech sitting up in the driver side of the Tahoe. Even after nine shots to the head and chest, he never slumped over. Niggas say he loved that Tahoe.

Bo yelled, "Fuck you doin', Fat Boy?"

Fat Joe looked at Ski and grabbed his stomach, throwing up.

The police sirens drew closer.

"Fat Boy, go get some help, muthafucka!" Bo kicked the truck hysterically.

"Somebody already called 911. I'm out—I just came home last week." Fat Boy went to stand on the sidewalk, his body trembling.

Dundee ran inside, holding his arm. "Goddamn, this shit burnin'." He grabbed the phone and dialed Poppa. "Yo, shit just popped off out the Lakes. Don't go out there. I'm headed over to Bayside."

Poppa heard the doorbell ringing and knocks banging in the background. "What happened?"

"Hold on." Dundee reached under his couch and pulled out his shotgun. He pulled his curtains back and saw Teisha, his baby momma.

"You drivin'?"

"Yeah. What happened?"

"I'll tell you in the car. Let's go to Bayside."

"Poppa!" Dundee climbed in the Honda Civic.

"Yeah. Talk, nigga!" Poppa said impatiently.

"Me and Tech was out the Lakes after you dropped me off. Rome, his clique, and Bo blocked us in and jumped out. I got a couple of them, and I think Tech, Rome, Ski, and Fat Boy dead. I don't know. Bo had two burners blastin' on me and I barely got away."

"Fat Boy and—" was all Teisha could get out her mouth before Dundee signaled for her to shut up.

"A'ight," Poppa said. "I'll holla back." Poppa knew he would catch the real story later out the Lakes.

"Now what was you gettin' ready to say?"

"I was tryin' to tell you that Rome ain't dead and Fat Joe was in the back on the floor. He didn't get touched. Ski dead, Tech dead, and the house next to the end, on the right, the lady's son got hit while playin' PlayStation. One of y'all niggas shot through the window. His momma was out there screamin' until the paramedics had to calm her down. They out there saying that the lady saw you and know you, and was talking to the police."

"I didn't shoot through no windows, and I didn't jump out first—fuck her! That was Rome punk ass."

"Don't matter. I just want you to know what Poppa gonna hear out the Lakes, so get your shit straight." Tiesha was young, but she knew guys died everyday. And she didn't want her baby daddy ending up dead.

She reached the emergency room.

"Why you didn't park?"

"I got to get home—my moms babysittin'."

"Park the fuckin' car. You goin' with me; yo' momma will be a'ight. I'll give her something later, shittt!!!"

"You gonna stop talkin' to me like you fuckin' crazy. You coulda got one of your other bitches to bring you up here." She got out the car.

"Keep talkin'. You in the right place to be runnin' your mouth—they can admit your ass real quick."

"You can call me later with all that bullshit you talkin' . . . 'cause I'm goin' home—you ain't admittin' me nowhere, muthafucka."

He put his good arm around her neck. "Shut the hell up. When I'm done, I'm gonna call you to come get me, so stay by the fuckin' phone."

Chapter Seven

Dee woke up to Tricia pushing her ass against his dick. *Damn*, he thought. He had just fucked when he came in. He knew them niggas had a good time with them shorties after he'd left them at the hotel and took the drive back to Tricia's crib. He felt like chilling, but he knew he'd be leaving for VA soon and wanted to give her some time.

After taking that Ecstasy he wasn't only ready to get freaked, but he was ready to suck titties, eat pussy, suck toes, lick ass. He smiled and put his arms around her. He was glad he had her to come home to. Vianna would've woke up, fucked, but no freakin'. And the thought of going to Chantel's house at three in the morning tryin' to fuck was out of the question.

Tricia was different. She appeared to be ready all the time—maybe not all the time, but he couldn't remember her ever telling him no.

The movement of her full, soft ass on his now-hard dick had him starting to move himself. He reached down and rubbed her thigh and ran his hand to the back of her left knee, and the left leg came up, giving him the perfect position to slide into a world that felt like a fantasy. He'd never felt a woman so soft, her body melted into his while he squeezed her in his arms.

Tricia didn't have the schooling and degrees that Chantel and Vianna had, but she had common sense and could relate to a man's struggle and mistakes. She also knew that the small things mattered, like cooking, bringing a glass of water, keeping a clean house—everything to make a man feel like a man. And she worked full-time and raised her daughter, never missing a beat when it came to him.

He pulled her tighter as his body began to let loose.

She pressed her ass against him and squeezed her pussy to drain him of every drop, then turned to him and kissed him. "I love you."

For Dee it was hard. He loved Tricia and Vianna, but his feelings for Chantel went much deeper—you could say borderline unconditional.

Tricia walked to the bathroom and returned with a wet, warm bathcloth. She wiped his dick thoroughly as he laid back happier than life.

His brother was back, he had a show tonight, and he had the support and an abundance of love from three strong, black women that made him feel like a king; women that any man in his right mind would kill for.

He leaned over and pulled his phone off his pants to call the hotel.

Kev answered the phone. "What the deal?"

"Nothin', fam. Where Strong?"

"In the bathroom."

"Tell him I'm headed back that way."

"A'ight." Kev walked to the bathroom. "He said drive the beamer."

"A'ight, one!" *Why the fuck he got me driving that old-ass, raggedy shit? Got a new Benz and I still got to fuck with that shit.* Dee complained, but nothing had changed—when Black said do something he had his reason and meant what he said.

Dee showered and got dressed. Tricia had to be to work at nine, so they left out together.

When Dee arrived at the hotel, Black was in the restaurant eating breakfast.

"So how much we need down for a new beamer? And how much a month?—I know you checked."

Dee smiled and said quickly, "Eight thousand down and trade-in worth twenty-five thousand, leaves us financing fifty thousand."

"Don't smile, nigga. We ain't got no real dough yet, but let's ride and look at one."

After eating they climbed in the car and shot up to Sandy Springs.

Dee had already checked out a new one with the dreams of getting two shows back-to-back and making the ten gees. Then the next move, without hesitation—put it all on the whip. Dee learned early that the status you put out there for self could put you where you needed to be; the rest was up to the hustle in your ass.

They pulled up to the BMW lot on the corner of Roswell and Abernathy. "Check that shit out, second from the left." Dee pointed and smiled.

They walked over to the BMW.

"What up, my brother?" the car salesman said, walking out with keys to the deep-burgundy 750iL, V-12. See you made it back."

Dee asked, "Same deal still on paper?"

"Ready! Pass me some dough and the title and we're in business."

Dee got the title out the car, and they walked into the office for Mike, the car salesman, to do the paperwork.

After about half an hour, Mike returned. "All I need is to call your job and get verification and some recent pay stubs."

Strong looked at Dee, hoping his brother was still on point.

Dee picked up the phone and called Vianna at work.

"Hello."

"Yes, Ms. Gonzalez, this is Arthur DeAndre Brooks. I'm trying to purchase a vehicle, and they need job verification and a copy of my last paycheck voucher. I have a fax number."

"Dee, I'm tied up right now," Vianna said; "I'll do it in a little bit."

"Yes, I need that done ASAP, thank you."

"Dee, I can't, right now."

Dee got up and stepped outside of Mike's office. "What the fuck! I can't really talk in the office. I'm up here now gettin' ready to get my shit and you jivin'. Goddamn! Take twenty minutes and do this please."

"All right." Vianna slammed the phone down. *Selfish-ass nigga. When he need me I'm suppose to jump, but when I ask him, he always too busy or broke. And he know this shit takes more than twenty fuckin' minutes.*

Dee and Strong were outside sitting in the four-door burgundy whip, sitting on aluminum rims, with a slight tint.

"So where you find out about dude?" Strong asked.

"Through you, nigga. You remember that nigga Ant from Portsmouth you use to fuck with back in the day?"

"Ant? The only Ant I know fuck with that diesel."

"Run with that nigga Lou from Tidewater Park. Well, I seen him at the strip joint. Kicked it a minute and the nigga was pushing a new 745il, and those shits ain't even hit the fuckin' streets. Got him a mini-mansion down here and everything. I got the nigga number."

"Gotta holla at him before I get out of here. He mighta came up. Really came up. Shit . . . I use to serve his peoples. He always been a hustler. Run hard. Last I heard he was sniffin' boy and robbin' niggas."

"Shit!" Dee said. "He must be robbin' a lot of niggas, because dude livin' well."

By this time Mike came out and let them know everything was a go.

Dee and Strong pulled off the lot in the new '99 BMW. When Dee pulled onto GA400 and punched it. "Hell yeah, nigga! Love you, man."

"I know, nigga. Let's get Lo and Kev. Go get the 500 and get to the mall. I can tell you need some new shit." Black handed Dee two stacks of hundreds and fifties equaling up to about five gees. He knew his brother had been through hell; scrambling around just like he was in New York. "Take care of your business here, man, so we can get outta here tomorrow. Find Ant number too."

"You got gear? That shit tonight at 201 Courtland is dress, son."

"I'll get something, but if Lo and Kev can't get in with Timbs and jeans, you know they ain't fuckin' with it."

After leaving Lennox Mall, Lo and Kev wanted to check the Underground that they'd heard so much about. Dee had to go handle business for the show, and Strong strolled along.

"Slow down, son. I got proper ID, but I ain't tryin' to use it."

"Bet. Just enjoyin' this shit. Damn near forgot how this feel. I got to pick dude up at the airport at seven, and this traffic gettin' ready to get fucked up."

Dee got on the phone and called Tricia. "Can you get off early today? Look, go home and I'll pick you up in twenty minutes."

When he arrived Tricia was pulling up in her '88 Dodge Aries, with smoke coming from under the car like she needed to be stopped. She saw Dee driving the new 750 BMW, and a wide smile came across her face. She climbed in and poked her lips out for Dee to kiss her.

Strong and Dee both knew public affection was a no-no, but Dee kissed her anyway.

Strong knew this bitch had his brother. *Why not? He seemed happy with her.*

Dee turned into the Jeep lot.

Strong shook his head smiling. "Dude said with

your credit and job, you could get that blue joint with a *G* down, right?"

"Yeah." Tricia smiled from ear to ear.

They got out and walked inside.

Thirty minutes later, Tricia was leaving the lot with thirty-day tags, looking fly as hell in her new, little four-door truck.

"I got the show tonight; I want you there. Here's five hundred. Get you something nice. Real nice. Show niggas who this VA nigga really is. Oh, and get some shit for the crib so I know y'all all right while I'm gone. I'm out tomorrow."

The wide smile disappeared. She knew her man was on his way back up and there was no way she could stop the hustle. She knew from past experiences, when you fuckin' with a street nigga, it's dough, the streets, and you—in that order.

Dee and Black headed towards the airport to pick up the night's featured artist.

"Yeah, on paper this nigga cost fifteen gees, but he used to hustle in VA back in the day with Dre. You know dude in the wheelchair from Up Top? So you know I hollered, got in contact with his manager. Half that.

"One day I want a phat-ass crib here. Then I can take niggas by the house. Real niggas we know. Most niggas in this lifetime don't even know I got a brother."

"I'm about that paper, Dee. It's always been 'get this money and have a good time,' but now it's 'get this money carefully and smart, then live good.' I know Ant got that diesel."

Dee told him, "We don't fuck with that shit—goddamn heroin!"

"Yeah, I know. I just want to holla."

"I hear yah. I already made that call. He'll be at the club tonight."

Strong gave Dee a pound. As always they were on the same page. "This ain't a bad city; it's relaxin', and it feels mad peaceful."

"Man, I thought I was the only muthafucka that felt that shit. This shit is relaxin' as hell. Like you ain't got a worry in the fuckin' world."

They arrived at the airport and picked up the artist and his manager. Dee had reserved them a suite at the same hotel they were in.

"This one wasn't bad," Dee said walking into their suite.

Kev had hooked his PlayStation up to the hotel television and was smoked-out, and Lo was tooted up and sipping on that Hen-dog, playin' NBA 2000.

"Usually niggas flow with an entourage and need a thousand things. All that nigga asked for was a bottle of Moët, two boxes of Dutch, and an ounce of that good green and he straight. And he'll leave for the club when we head out for the club."

"How they goin'?" Lo asked. "They got any ice on."

"Bitch niggas better get they ass in a fuckin' cab." Kev looked at Dee and pulled out his bag of X. "Yo, big brother, how you feel?"

"Good, son, but I'm about to get better." Dee took one with some orange juice.

Strong passed him the Backwoods.

Dee took a long drag, "Usually I rent a limo, but it's only two niggas. And what's better than pulling in front of the club in a new 740 and a new 500?"

"Yeah, but I've seen some shit down here."

Dee told him, "And you ain't seen shit. Wait 'til tonight. Niggas comin' out with it. See, in the ATL you got ballin'-ass niggas battlin' with those music niggas and those professional ballplayin' niggas. Everybody tryin' to live like they got ballplayin' money. But a lot niggas got dough."

"Should be plenty of bitches for every muthafuckin' nigga who want to fuck, all these gay-ass niggas I seen," Kev said. "Me and Lo went roamin' around today; we seen gay-ass niggas everywhere.

"ATL got the largest population of gay black men. They come in packs. They say that some gay niggas like to act like thugs. They put gold fronts in they mouth, loose jeans on and white T's, like they playin' thug, but all along they want to pack meat in they ass. Kev, please tell me you don't pack meat. Oh Lord!" Dee yelled out, laughing along with everybody else.

Dee looked at Kev seriously as Lo and Strong looked on. "Check this, little brother. I want to tell you two things, and remember your big brother told you this. One—always be yourself. Fuck the world if they can't adjust. If those bullshit fronts were you, they would be permanently attached. Two—never fuck with a bitch who can't do shit for you. I mean, really hold you down and got her shit together. Fuck with shorties that got credit, credit cards, bank accounts and good credit, not those bitches who let niggas in their past fuck their shit up with cars and cribs. Hoes like that, you know their past and where they been. So what type of bitches you think you gonna attract with those bullshit fronts in your mouth? Nigga, I will never tell you nothin' wrong. Promise you that."

Dee went to shower and get dressed. When he returned he stepped wearing beige slacks, dark brown Cole Haan's with a gold buckle, and a dark-brown button-down. He changed his clear eyeglasses to some slightly tinted Ralph Lauren framed glasses.

"Now, what kind of bitches am I gonna attract?" Dee grabbed the Backwoods and gave Kev and Lo a pound. "Hurry up, Strong. Got to get to the club so they don't fuck up my money.

Strong came out wearing black, wool, pleated Coogi slacks and a black Coogi sweater and some black square-toed Prada shoes, set off by a stainless steel Breitling timepiece, not to mention the clear, platinum-framed Gucci glasses.

"Somebody, pop that nigga collar," Lo said.

Dee looked at Strong, thinking how his little brother done stepped the club gear up.

"I clubbed a little in the city," Strong said, checking his gear.

"These niggas jigged the fuck up," Kev said without his fronts, smiling and revealing the prettiest set of white teeth.

"I got on Dickies, new white T and new Timbs—shit, I'm dressed," Lo said.

They headed over to the club. When they pulled in front of 201 Courtland, the line was already forming. The artist jumped out of the S500 driven by Dee. Strong was in the back chilling, sipping on Henny XO, and smoking that Gandi the artist had requested.

The artist's manager decided to roll with Lo, wanting a toot before his night got popping.

Dee felt good. Not only was he in control of the night's show, but this was the last time fuckin' with niggas outside the family.

"Yo, I forgot to tell y'all something," Dee yelled over the music.

They all leaned in.

"Being it's so many gay niggas down here, it's an abundance of females. They always outnumber us—this shit gonna be off the hook."

Security tapped Dee on the shoulder and talked in his ear.

Tricia was there with two friends. They all had the fellas' attention when they flowed in. Tricia walked up and hugged Dee.

"Heah, Strong," she said smiling.

She continued, "This is Lo, Kev, and Strong, and these are my girlfriends, Kay and Sheronna."

Black stared over at the back room where the artist was relaxing. Lo was bouncing around with two Heinekens.

Kev stared at Dee. They were both feeling the X. Dee cut his eye at Kay, telling Kev that he probably could, knowing Kay liked pretty-ass niggas.

"Let me get y'all a drink," Kev suggested, and of course, they agreed. "We'll need to get a bottle and pop some champagne so the head can get right."

"Tell them to bring it to the table," Dee said as he guided them to the back room that had couches, tables, and its own bar.

As the club began to pack, four females walked

to the front, cutting line. "Don't act like you don't know who the fuck I am—I got most of y'all niggas money in my pocket," Peaches said. Her crew started laughing.

Dee saw them and signaled for security to let them through.

"What up, Dee?" Ecstasy asked.

"Coolin', baby," he said kissing Ecstasy, Peaches, Star, and Diamond, four of the baddest bitches ATL had to offer—faces perfect, bodies perfect, nails, hair, and feet, all done to perfection.

Dee met these girls when he started doing shows. They worked at Strokers, a gentleman's club. They had approached him, letting him know for any stars that wanted real women, they were his connect and he always got a kickback.

Out of nowhere Ant came strolling up, hype, giving security and the owner pounds. He gave Dee a pound and stared down the clique.

"Do me a favor, Ant—see the girls to the back so they can meet the artist. Yo, Black in the back too."

All these bitches had tight bodies, Dee thought, *but not one of them had shit on Tricia.*

Everybody who had VIP was in the back room behind a rope—Lo, Kev, Strong, Tricia, her friends, the artist, Peaches and her crew, the investors and their team and their girls. For every bottle the investors bought, Lo and Kev got a bottle with Strong's nod. The artist lit a Dutch, which triggered a chain reaction. The investor team lit up, Kev lit up, and the party began. The artist's manager told the girls that Kev had that shit to get you "rolling" and Lo had that "soft." Before long the VIP was banging.

The investors wondered who these cats were. They could tell Strong was the money because of his attire, style, and how Kev and Lo ran shit past him.

Two of the girls who were supposed to be working the artist, Diamond and Star, made their way over to Strong and Ant as they kicked it about Tidewater and the early 90's.

Ant saw the investors and his team order four bottles of Moët. He called the waitress who was taking Lo's order. "Bring two bottles of Cristal for me and my man, some glasses, twenty shots of Henny, ten 'thug passions' for all these hoes, and ten Heinekens."

Lo signaled for the waitress to cancel his order.

"Show these Southern muthafuckas how VA niggas get down." Ant gave Strong a pound.

"They don't know." Lo let out the "LE yell," rolling his tongue with the *L* and letting the *E* flow. Then he took his T-shirt and wrapped it around his head like a turban.

Strong knew he was now fucked up. *No matter where you carry a Lake Edward nigga, he'll be LE to the heart, 'til he ain't breathin' no more, never steppin' out of character for nobody.*

Dee came back to the VIP followed by Ken-Ken. They grabbed glasses for the champagne. "You remember my brother Strong," Dee said, allowing Strong and Ken-Ken to give each other a pound.

Ken-Ken swore his name was Black, but he knew his face and reputation. Him and Ant knew each other from school, growing up in Portsmouth, and Ken-Ken knew his reputation. Ken-Ken didn't hustle, he was a barber and a cool-ass barber, known for cutting all the hustlers' heads and was a made middleman, fitting in and never responsible for anything.

Dee grabbed the *L* from Kev and introduced Ken-Ken. "This is my cousin Lo, and this my little brother Kev."

"I ain't know you had another brother."

"He was too young then; now he think he grown, hangin' with the big boys." Dee punched Kev lightly in the chest.

"How you feelin'?" Kev asked.

"What?" Dee had a wide grin.

Kev reached in his pocket and pulled out his bag.

Dee grabbed two. "I want shorty to try this shit at least once."

Kev handed him another one. "Give this to Kay for me."

Dee pulled Tricia away from the crowd. "You a'ight?" He passed her the Backwoods.

She hugged him. "Yes, I'm wonderful."

"Things gettin' ready to get much better. Hold me down, and I'll always play fair and be here."

"You never have to worry." She stared into his eyes. Her tongue ring just took sexiness to another level.

"Yo, try this."

"What is it?" She took it from him.

"*X*—so you can say you tried it and you won't ever try this shit with nobody else. I wouldn't give you shit to fuck with you."

"They were takin' them earlier. Kay and Sheronna wanted to try one too."

"Well, Kev said to give this to Kay. Give it to her on the sly—no more freebies." Dee watched Tricia walk away, and the way her ass shook with every step. *Goddamn*!

Dee was standing beside Kev in the crowd while the artist put on his show. Kev told him, "It's some hoes in here."

"It's like this everyday all day and night in the ATL," Dee replied. "But you know, hoes or not, Strong can adapt to any environment. The nigga changes with the times. He has no choice." Dee looked around for his brother. He knew Black was wanted by the Feds and had been running a long time. That's why he never questioned Black about the way he wanted to handle things, like his own security, and anybody that jeopardized that, without a question, would rest forever.

Tricia, Kay, and Sheronna came up. Tricia stood in front of Dee, allowing her ass to rest on his lap as she danced to the artist.

Kay hyped her up and egged her on, both high off the weed, drunk from the thug passion and champagne, all while rolling off the *X*. Kay stood in front of Kev with her jeans so tight, Kev saw every curve in her perfectly shaped ass.

Kev touched her waist and pulled her to him. He knew she was on it, he had to make sure nothing else pulled him in. She was phat to death, and with him rolling and her rolling, the touches between the two became very arousing and intense as they moved around as one.

Dee knew the deal—Tricia kept turning around,

talking about how good she felt. Dee tried to hold his eyes open and calm his racing body down. *Damn! I feel good as shit*, he thought.

The artist finished, and they escorted him out the door. The 740 made the escape back to the hotel, carrying Kev, the artist, and his manager, followed by Peaches and her team. They got to the hotel, Dee and Kev headed to the suite after giving pounds to the artist and his manager.

Moments later, there was a knock at the door. Kev jumped up, and Dee laid a magazine over the 'dro he was getting ready to roll.

"Who the hell is that?"

"Strong and Lo wasn't leavin' the club, right? Ain't we goin' back?" Kev walked to the door.

"Yeah! I'm goin' back, then I'm headed to the Dec and catch up with my baby."

"With-my-baby, gay-ass nigga."

Dee knew he sounded soft, but he was talking about Tricia and didn't give a fuck.

"Yo, it's those hoes," Kev said in a low voice.

"Who?" Dee walked over and peeped through the hole and opened the door. "Fuck y'all doin' here?"

"They ain't doin' shit. Just chillin' one-on-one and Star said she had to tell Kev something."

"Fuck you got to tell my little brother?" Dee said as he finished rolling. "What y'all get out of them niggas?"

"Thirty-five hundred." Diamond gave Dee fifteen hundred. "Ecstasy and Peaches in the suite gettin' tip money."

"Y'all did good. Five hundred apiece for comin'

to the club and makin' a nigga feel like he famous and shit." Dee lit the Backwoods.

The night was a success. He'd made forty thousand and he'd pocketed eight gees and he made money with his girl clique. They always hit him off and showed their appreciation for letting them in on the stars he brought in. He never worried about them cheating him, because they knew for a nigga to get four bad-ass bitches in Atlanta to replace them was easy as picking up the phone.

Diamond moved closer to Dee. "I'm tryin' to get my tip."

"Girl, you better double up on Kev," Dee said seriously.

She rested her body against his, then grinded her pelvis against his dick.

He ran his hand down her back, slowly down her spine, to the nape of her back. He rubbed the thin, soft material that clung to her ass to reveal every enticing curve. He felt the thong and followed it from the top until it disappeared into the crack of her ass. His dick was instantly hard.

She backed up and removed the dress and stood on the bed in just the lavender thong. She turned around and began to make her ass jump. She then faced Dee on her knees, pointed her finger, and signaled for him to come closer.

He approached her.

She unzipped his pants and pulled out his dick. She ran her tongue across the tip.

He thought he was going to scream.

She slowly took it in and sucked like a pro.

Dee looked over at Kev, he was putting on a condom getting ready to throw something in Star, who had her knees planted into the couch with her red ass high in the air, exposing all her love, which gave Dee's dick some extra stiffness.

When they finished tricking, they threw the girls two hundred for their tip. They burst out and headed back to the club, where Lo and Strong were in the front by the 500 with two shorties.

"We headed to Tricia's. I got to go find my baby Kay." Kev pulled up by where Lo and Strong were chillin'.

Strong smiled. Lo was sitting in the passenger side, head laid back, eyes shut, fucked up.

"Yo, we out 9:00," Strong said.

"Bet. I'll holla," Dee yelled.

Kev threw up the peace sign headed towards Decatur.

They arrived at Tricia's. Candles were lit up and she had just gotten out the shower.

Kay was on the couch smoking. "Where the fuck you was with my man?" she asked Dee, grabbing Kev's hand.

Dee and Tricia started laughing.

"We'll see y'all in the morning." Kev smiled and went out the door. Kay lived in the same complex.

It was 9:00 on the nose when Kev and Dee pulled in front of the hotel. Lo and Strong were already ready to go. "Gotta stop at Vianna's, and we out."

"Following you."

They left and ran by Vianna's. She was up cooking breakfast while her child looked at cartoons, already dressed.

"What's going on?"

"Fine. I'm going to Northgate Mall, then I'm going by Barnes and Nobles down the street to find a couple of children's books and pick up my book club book of the month."

"What type of bullshit y'all readin' this month?" Dee asked.

"Actually, we're taking a different turn, instead of the norm. Somebody suggested we try one of those street novels. The girl said it was 'hard' street—you might enjoy it, something you might relate to, 'cause I can't. It's called *My Time To Shine* and it's about the streets of Virginia."

"Fuck readin'—somebody need to write a book about me and my family's life and the hell we been through. That's a goddamn story. Best fuckin' seller. I'll look at a movie, but fuck readin' shit."

"Do you know how you sound?"

"I don't give a *f-u-u-u-c-k*."

"I'm also going to stop by my job for about an hour. Are you gonna be here when I get back?"

Dee looked at her hating that he had to leave. She was being sweet, not fussing and that's when she had his heart.

"Naw, I got to go to VA."

She looked startled because she knew VA was off limits, he had his moms there, but he was in and out, never a day. "How long?"

"Couple weeks. Putting some things together." He reached in his pocket. "I need to put this in the business account." He gave her two gees. "And this is your two hundred and eight hundred for you to buy yourself something. He pulled her to him and hugged her.

She squeezed him tight.

"Walk me out?" Dee turned to her daughter. "And you be good."

They walked outside.

She saw the beamer. "Ummm, oh! When were you going to tell me? Damn, that's nice. So my baby doin' his thing." She moved closer. She knew this was Black's doing. She just bowed her head and said a silent prayer. She hugged Dee and whispered in his ear, "I love you. Please be careful and call me soon."

"I will, and you be good." He started up the 740.

"You know you don't got shit to worry about," she said with an attitude as if he'd said something real stupid.

Dee didn't ever worry about another nigga getting no pussy. It took him a second to find out she really fucks off her emotions, so another man never crossed his mind. Women were another story.

Dee met her four years ago, but she had chosen an alternate lifestyle. They were friends and they did business together, but the last three years something clicked and she was all into him, but she always said if it didn't work out she was going back to "The Life."

He watched as she made her way back to her door. "Boy, you just don't know."

"Naw, nigga, you fuckin' your pimp game up. You really care about your girls; you ain't no playa." Kev laughed.

"You right about that, my nigga. You right about that."

* * *

Three hours later they pulled in front of Chantel's house. Dee walked up and went inside. "Y'all, hold tight. Let me make sure she straight.

"Chantel!"

"Heah, baby?" She wrapped her arms around him. "You have company with you?"

"Yeah, my peoples."

"Hold on. Let me go put on something." She put down her books and went into the bedroom.

Chantel was the woman—strong, confident, and sexy as they come. He watched as her large breast moved in slow motion through her shirt and her nipples got hard and poked through. He could feel his soft penis begin to erect.

He looked as the T-shirt clung to her full, low-cut panties. Her body was not soft, but toned, her breasts large with thick, dark nipples.

He went to the door and signaled for them to come in. He walked into the room.

She had removed her shirt and was leaning over to come out her panties. Dee grabbed her, hugged her and gave her a kiss.

She kissed him, then pulled away and got in the shower. "How things go last night?" she yelled loudly from the shower.

"Fine. I came off a'ight—five gees."

"I heard that. You know you got shit to take care of. You got two tickets and a fine that gots to be paid. You charged six fifty on the VISA and we need to put that four hundred in the mail like yesterday for your child support—before they pick your ass up. All that come to about twelve hundred."

"I got that."

"Well, big money, you got five hundred for my maintenance? It's time. I need four hundred for my credit card bills and a thousand for shopping." Chantel laughed. She spread more lotion on her body.

Dee walked over. He put lotion on his hands and began spreading it on her back.

She turned around.

He took her large breast in his hand and placed her nipple in his mouth.

"Stop, they in the livin' room."

"So?—they ain't in here."

"Dee, you better—"

He laid her aback and put her clit between his lips and sucked, his tongue flicking across her clit lightly. Ten minutes of strong sucking, licking, flickering, heavy panting and she was squeezing his head between her legs.

He eased on top of her, allowing his dick to slide into her soaking wet, extremely warm pussy. He closed his eyes in ecstasy without being on Ecstasy. He pumped in and out with a feeling that you only get from new pussy and love.

She moved her body with his every stroke. As her body began to climax, she brought her legs up and back so that his strokes would rub against her clit, her vagina grabbing at his dick, pulling.

His body began to tremble, as the greatest feeling in the world raced from his feet to his head, and went numb.

They got dressed. Dee laid three thousand on the dresser—all the money he'd made. He knew this shit was coming back, running over. He had to handle his shit and make sure she was okay before he burst.

Chantel smiled. She knew this was the work of Black. Dee never had no extra, not like this . . . except for when she met him. Now she was getting ready to lose him to the streets again and she couldn't take it.

"I got to go to VA."

She knew this was coming.

They walked outside. She spoke to the same team that had knocked on her door two days ago.

Strong held up her book. "So how much longer?"

"Another year and a half and I'll have my doctorate."

"Bachelor's, easy; master's, real hard. This shit here is a whole lot of writing. Sometimes I want to say fuck it, but I came too far."

"Don't we know," Dee added.

They all walked outside.

She shook her head at the new BMW with Georgia tags.

He gave her the keys. "I'll be back in a couple weeks. You know I'll call you." He kissed her. Then they climbed in the 500 and were out.

"I know she get lonesome down here by herself," Kev said.

"She work and go to school full-time. She don't give or take out too much time for nothing else . . . including me."

Dee loved Chantel more than anything. She had proven she would be there through anything, but she never catered to his every need. But she was always there.

She dished sex out as if it was a bill, once a week if that. But he understood. She was caught up in her studies and work, *but goddamn!*

Even though Vianna and Tricia were wonderful women, Dee felt without Chantel, his world would definitely crumble. He couldn't make it without her and didn't want to try. She inspired him, gave him that "get up and go," and the thoughts of giving her the world was what kept him striving hard all these years. Her dreams were his; his dreams were hers—she was his world.

Chapter Eight

Where the fuck is Shannon? Angela stood in front of the MCI Building in Alpharetta, GA (some say North Atlanta). This was the third time this week she'd been late. *She knows I want to go home before I go to the club.* Angela began to walk up the sidewalk in the heels and hot pants suit. *This is some bullshit.*

She came down here with Shannon, but she got the money together to get the apartment, dancing. Now she got this job during the day. *Shannon's not doing nothing, but running her car in the fucking ground. I know she's going to give me that "got-caught-in-traffic" shit. I'm going to start keeping my shit. Then she'll really be stuck.* Then she saw her car pull around the corner. She climbed in.

Shannon headed towards 400S. As they made their way down 400, the traffic was bumper to bumper. "I ran into that shit, tryin' to get to Exit 9."

"Should have left earlier. You got more time, and I'll be drivin' my own shit."

"Come on, chill." Shannon put her hand on Angela's leg. "You hungry?"

"Yeah!"

"What you want?" Shannon was talking like she had money.

Angela noticed the new sweatsuit, sneakers, and headband and the bulge in Shannon's pocket. She reached down and grabbed it. "Where you get this?"

Before Angela could get it out, Shannon slaps the shit out of her. "Bitch, don't you ever."

Angela yelled, punching Shannon.

Shannon grabbed her hands, trying to stop her—*Bam*!!!!! They ran into the back of a Chrysler Concord.

"Now look what you did. What the fuck we goin' to do?" Shannon yelled.

"What the fuck am *I* going to do? I'm the one that got to get to work," Angela said with tears beginning to fall down her face.

Traffic began to back up. They got out the car to assess the damage. There was no question about whose fault it was—Shannon received a ticket, and the car was towed away.

Shannon and Angela were dropped by the tow company closer to home. Then they caught a cab from a wreckage company off I20. The cab cost twenty-two dollars by the time they got to their apartment on the West End.

Angela walked in her door. "How the fuck am I going to get to the club? I'm late, but I damn sure can't be a no-show, I'll get fired."

"We'll catch a cab and figure out all this transportation shit later."

* * *

They arrived at Strokers at 9:00, two hours after Angela was supposed to be on the floor at 7:00. She quickly changed, tooted her two lines, and headed for the floor, wearing light-green, skin-tight shorts that left over half her ass hangin' out.

She strolled out and glanced around. Many had their money in hand, giving her the signal. She caught glimpse of a fifty and the knot he tried not to expose. She eased her way over. Her large firm breasts barely swayed, but her ass bounced with every movement. She began to dance sensually and removed her shorts.

By the time she left that table, two hundred was made off two songs. *Those were real niggas.*

Her night was about to end when Shannon pulled out a twenty, and Angela came over and began to dance.

Shannon knew she had Angela, but she knew Angela came from a man's world and she always had one. But she made her feel for a woman—that she knew would be in Angela forever. She also knew Angela was about dough. She looked into Angela's eyes as Angela stared back slowly moving her body to the music. Shannon loved the twenty-one-year-old young woman she turned out. She was all Angela knew about the life, and she was planning on keeping her ass in eyesight and locked down.

Angela slid her pants on, gathered her money, headed for the dressing room. A dark-skinned brother grabbed her hand. "Please dance for me?" he said, holding out two fifty-dollar bills.

She could see the gold crowns on the four front teeth. In just that one sentence, she also knew he wasn't from GA.

She began to dance.

Shannon stared. *When her time was up she always flew off the floor. Why did this nigga catch her attention? How much did he give her?*

Angela couldn't keep her eyes off him. She looked at the tattoos that ran up his forearms. It had been a long time since she'd even desired a man, but this cat's vibe was real. She looked at the guy that sat in the booth beside him. She'd seen him many times in her two months there. He had even tried to take her out, talking about he was VA's finest in the ATL. She never entertained their conversation; she never entertained anyone's conversation—especially the other bitches that always tried to get at her. *Ant—that's his name, but who is this guy beside him?*

"What's your name?" the guy asked.

"Champagne."

"Fuck that—what's your name?"

She blurted, "Angela," before she knew it. She'd never told anybody her name because it was all a game.

"I'm Strong." He passed her a card with his numbers on it. "If something happens to this card for any reason, remember Triple Strong Entertainment. Call information. Leave a message, work number, e-mail or something."

Angela looked at him.

"I'll be here until tomorrow, then I'm out. And

if I were trying to fuck, I would offer you a couple grand and skip the bullshit."

Strong was back in ATL. He'd come down to handle some business with Ant. It took them almost two months before Ant decided to pull him in. Strong got his enterprise popping with the backing of Polite, and things were running well. Strong's plan was to try and find Bo's connect, so Poppa could control all of that. But Dundee had set off shit and things were off the hook, but with Dee handling the apartments for lookouts, and the real estate out Lake Edward for stash spots, a fortress was being built.

Poppa had runners, workers, and "watch out" niggas all reporting straight to him, Lo, and Kev, who had learned the land.

Strong was bringing in the weight, and it was getting moved fast. Mont and Speed were working out perfectly.

Poppa was having problems trying to put his people on the other side since Rome got shot up. Bo was on a vengeance. When Dundee set off the gunplay, it left three people dead, but left Rome fucked up. He could no longer stand on his own. He had to use the help of handicap tilts. No longer the young man he used to be, he couldn't control his bladder and walked around wearing a bag. It fucked Bo up every time he saw his brother.

The day he picked up Rome was a glorious day as they left Norfolk General Hospital. He pulled in the front as they rolled his brother down. He had hired a home-care nurse to sit in his home and take care of Rome. Rome sat on the passenger side in silence. Bo knew it wasn't much to say. This was something Rome was going to have to come to grips with. He'd lived his life avoiding shit like this, but now he got caught up early in the game and it was tragic. It hurt him to see his brother like this.

As he pulled out of the hospital parking lot, he never paid the men in black suits with bowties any attention as they approached his truck with the *Final Call.*

"Would you like the *Final Call,* my brother?" the guy in the Muslim suit asked.

"Or some incense or oils?" the other one asked the passenger.

"Naw, I'm a'ight." Bo didn't want to be bothered.

"Can you make a donation, my brother?"

Bo reached in his pocket and held out a five for the guy. He never expected for the guy to grab his arm. When he realized what was going on it was too late—out came the nine that sat in the pack of *Final Call* newspapers—to his neck.

The second Muslim opened the door, picked up Rome, and threw him in the back, not giving a fuck how he landed. Rome let out a groan as he tried to adjust his twisted body.

One was in front with his burner on Bo, and the other Muslim climbed in the back with Rome.

They made Bo drive to a undisclosed location in the Industrial Park. "Shut off the engine, put your hands on the steering wheel." The guy secured Bo's hands to the steering wheel tightly.

They tied Rome's hands; his legs weren't much help to him at this time. Then they placed them both in seatbelts and secured them. Right about the same time a tinted-out, charcoal-grey 300M pulled up.

Black stepped from the car. Bo's already shaken stomach was now about to turn over. Piss trickled down his leg, and he clenched his ass tight, to control his bowels.

"So what's the deal, baby?" Black walked toward the truck and smiled at Bo.

"Come on, Black . . . I thought—I thought—"

"You thought I was never comin' back. You thought you had shit under control. You thought you could fuck me and it was never comin' back on ya. But you thought the wrong thought, partner."

Lo walked up.

"You was my man, Bo, and right now I can't even say anything in your defense. You fucked everybody that ever tried to do something for you."

Up pulled a black 929, tinted-out. Poppa got out the passenger side while Dundee parked. Dundee sat in the car (he finally got a chance to see the infamous Black). He was riding this nigga shirttail and he knew this cat was legendary.

"Bring that, Poppa?" Black asked.

"Yeah," Poppa said.

"Pop the trunk, Dun." he said as he approached the trunk. He pulled out a red gas container.

Bo eyes widened with fear.

Rome began to breathe hard. "*Uhh! Uhh! Uhh! Uhh!*" This was some shit he could have never imagined. He looked into Poppa eyes. "Please, Poppa, I never did nothing to deserve this. Come on, Lo. Oh! God. Help me!" Tears ran down his face.

Poppa walked over to the truck. They both began to yell as Poppa poured gas into the truck on Bo's lap, on the door, to the floor, soaked the seat around him. Bo began to go crazy, trying to break away from the steering wheel, but he was secured well. Them fake Muslims did their part and were long gone.

Black lit his already rolled Backwoods.

They watched as Poppa approached Rome's side and began pouring gas into his lap, floor, door and soaking the floor. He threw the container on the floor between them.

Rome was still crying and praying. "Jesus, please help me. Jesus, please. I'll be a child of yours forever, if you help me! Please, Lo. Please, Lo." He turned his head in Lo's direction.

"Better keep calling on Jesus because he's the only one that can help your ass now." Lo took a sip of the Hennessy.

Black looked into Bo's eyes. "This gay-ass, snitchin' muthafucka, sittin' here with slobber runnin' from his mouth and tears on his face, cryin', 'Oh God! Oh, Black! Oh, God! Oh Black!'" Black took a long pull off the Back, then flicked it inside the window.

The lower part of the car burst into flames. The screams ripped through Poppa, but he stood there.

This shit was an act of a beast. No man barbecues another human being, Dundee thought. He stared in amazement as their screams turned to sighs. This was a savage act, but Bo was a snitch and, inside, everybody out there knew this shit should have been done a long time ago. Dundee had nothing but respect for this nigga that now headed up the team.

Lo turned the pint of Hennessy up to his lips and gulped. Then he took the bottle and threw it, busting Bo in his now-cremated head. "Have some Henny, son—you had a good life."

They climbed in the whips and were headed back to The Lakes to claim their home.

In the three months Strong had been in VA, he moved over eighty kilos of cocaine through the seven cities. He was moving about six ki's a week, but for the last two weeks, ten bricks were being pushed out the door. He had a slight problem within his organization that had to be addressed. He'd seen Dundee at the mall in Hampton. Dee had gotten Strong a house in Hampton, away from it all. Before leaving VA, that was far, but after chilling in ATL, it wa'n' shit, as long as you had a nice whip.

Dundee came to him like a real hustler with respect. "I've only seen you a couple times, Strong, but I know who you are." Dundee gave him a pound.

Strong knew he was feeding this nigga.

"Can I holla at you a second?"

"Sure. Holla!"

"I'm movin' three bricks a week, some through my LE, some to my peoples in Carolina."

"What part?" Strong had some bad experiences with Carolina cats.

"Well, I'm from Elizabeth City originally. But I been out The Lakes since I can remember. My cousin's down there gettin' like I'm gettin' it, but they can't stay supplied. They are movin' from

Elizabeth City, goin' to Raleigh, Durham, Greensboro, and Charlotte. I can move five a week through them—they ready to buy—but I don't have it to buy and Poppa won't, or can't, front it. Which leaves that money I could be gettin' danglin' in the wind."

"I understand," Strong said. "I'll get back at you."

Dundee walked off not knowing if he'd done the right thing. *But how was he going to get back, he didn't have my number?*

Strong sat there thinking he had made over four hundred in three months. He was giving Polite fifteen gees for each brick, getting twenty gees or better. Here Ant was getting ready to give him twenty bricks for two hundred thousand and give a kilo of heroin for seventy-five thousand and a street value of one hundred eighty thousand.

Strong told Polite to see if he could match the love, but it wasn't possible. Strong even asked him if he wanted to come in and they get forty ki's.

Polite was ready for the move but said he still had to get to Memphis.

Ant yelled for another girl to come dance as Angela made her way through the door.

"So it's on, my nigga—VA niggas gettin' it," Ant said.

"How can you do it, though? How?"

Ant leaned over. He'd known Black a long time and he knew the nigga that sat in front of him was real. "I'm in bed with some Africans. I was in the wrong place at the wrong time, or you might say right time. I saw some shit go down. Africans was doin' a deal and the muthafucka cut dude hand off. They sliced his head in half and left the machete there. Pulled out burners and popped two more cats. I had left the 750 in a garage. I took off thinking I was straight. Two days later, cats are at my house. When I come in—the house I had then was nice but secluded. No cars, no idea—muthafuckas ask who am I. I know I'm gonna die," Ant looks at Black. He had Black's undivided attention even though fifty of the finest dancers in ATL were within inches, naked.

"Before I knew it, I was hemmed up with a wire around my neck, cuttin' my shit. Rippin', man. Then I told them, 'I'm from VA. I hustle heroin.' I had half a million in the garage and three ki's in the stash in the car. They got the heroin and the money . . . and let me down. They ask me about the muthafucka I dealt with and pulled us in. Now I'm a millionaire in this shit. They have unlimited supply of soft and that diesel. So let's get you rich and me richer.

Strong couldn't complain; he was getting ready to come off, but still had to move this diesel.

Chapter Nine

Angela walked in the door. Shannon followed her, complaining about the attention she'd given Strong. "Know what . . . you are gettin' sickenin'!"

"Now I'm sickenin'? Why is that now? You tore up my car, I'm sittin' here trying to figure out how I'm gettin' to work in the morning and you talkin' about a nigga." Angela went to the room to undress and to take a shower.

"I been watchin' you dance for months now. You never give anybody the time of day, nor do you take numbers. Where is the card anyway?" Shannon went through her things.

"Know what, Shannon . . ." Angela stood in front of her nude. ". . . we came down here together. The girl I met in VA was lovable and comforting. Now I don't need comforting—I'm past that—I need love, support, trust. Somebody to help me up and get myself together so I can bring Li'l D down here. And now that my car is fucked up, you're hinderin' me. Instead of tryin' to figure out how the problem is going to be resolved, or how I'm goin' to get to work and back to the club, you here wildin' out, throwin' my shit, and actin' like a fool."

Angela shook her head and walked into the shower. She allowed the water to wash the sweat and filth off her body. She could hear Shannon hollering. Shannon's babbling came closer. Then she heard the bathroom door open.

"Why you blamin' me for your faults? You aren't perfect, and you wrecked your shit, bitch. That's why your own cousin help me turn your ass out. I have been here for you when nobody else was, when you were runnin' around here fucked up because you had two muthafuckin' niggas killed for nothin'. Because you wanted to be a fuckin' ho."

Angela turned off the water and pulled back the curtain. "Now I know how you really feel."

"You bein' smart." Shannon stepped towards Angela and grabbed her hair.

Angela grabbed Shannon by the throat, but the force of Shannon pulling her hair slammed her to the tub. Angela began swinging.

Shannon got two grips on her head, trying to push it under the water in the slow-draining tub.

Flashbacks of Mac overpowering her, pushing her head underwater, came back to Angela, and she dug her nails into Shannon's face and eyes.

Shannon let go, and Angela's hands were swinging wild. Shannon's fight soon became a scramble to get away. She busted out the bedroom with Angela on her ass.

Angela slipped on the wet floor, coming up only

to grab the iron, twirling it, barely missing Shannon's head, and leaving a large imprint in the wall. She heard the front door slam.

Angela fell on the bed, trying to catch her breath. "God, why am I going through this bull-shit. Why?"

She grabbed her robe and went to run some bath water. She needed to sit in the tub and relax. She turned off all the lights and lit two candles. As her body hit the hot steaming water, she let out a long sigh. She held the phone in her hand. She wanted to call somebody. Her best male friends were dead.

Her heart fell as she thought about the day Monica called and told her about Rome. She had flown home to see him when he got shot up, and was lying in the hospital. There was no coming back when they found him and his brother damn near cremated. Her girlfriend, Monica, she just didn't want to hear her drama, and Trinity was another story.

She didn't know anybody in Atlanta, except for the people she worked with, and that was business. And she didn't really fuck with none of the dancers, except for one. She thought about the number 678-424-xxxx.

"Hello," the man's voice answered.

"Dream there?"

"Don't no muthafuckin' Dream live here. Dream worked at the club; call down there."

"Can I speak to Felicia?" she said with an atti-tude.

"The phone, Fee—it's one of those dike-ass, trick bitches you dance with," her friend said.

"Hello," Dream said.

"What the deal, girl? It's Champagne." Her and Angela had talked a few times, but not that often.

Dream was like her—she had another job and just danced strictly for the dough, not trying to get caught up in the money.

"Heah, girl! Sorry about my friend."

"See you kind of busy?"

"Hell no, girl. Just got out of the shower and he gettin' ready to carry his ass to work. That's why he mad. Got a job and still broke. I'd be mad too." Dream laughed.

"I just wanted somebody to holla at."

"Where your girl?"

"We fell out big—she left."

"That's why I don't get down with bitches. I've heard those hoes put you through more shit than a nigga. At least a nigga got something I can play with."

Her and Angela talked about twenty more minutes. "A'ight, Fee. See you tomorrow."

"Definitely. I go on at six, and Angela, take it for what it's worth—the life you livin' is a controversial life; if you want it to get better, get a man."

Angela climbed out the tub and dried off, thinking about what Dream said. She lotioned down and wrapped her head. Then she fell to her knees, something she hadn't done in a while, and began to pray. *It had to get better.*

The sound of the alarm clock scared Angela. Usually it was set for music, but somehow it ended on alarm. "Goddamn, I just laid the fuck down." She walked into the living room to see if Shannon was there. *I guess she found another bitch to lay up with.* She did want to know that she was all right. She reached for the phone and dialed 301-497-xxxx.

"Hello," Lenore answered.

"Heah, Lenore, can I speak to my dad?"

"Yeah," he said.

"Heah, Daddy. I miss you."

"What happen, baby?"

"I wrecked my car."

"You all right? Did you report it to your insurance?"

"Yes, yes. But I need to get a rental."

"Talk to Lenore. She'll send you something. Take care. I got to run."

"Dad, I also need a two-hundred-dollar deposit . . . because I'm not twenty-five."

"Damn, baby. Let me see what's up. Call me on my cell at noon."

Angela got dressed and headed to the Marta. She was going to have to ride to North Spring Station and catch the bus to MCI. *What the hell am I gonna do?*

She sat at her cubicle making calls, not being productive at all. Her mind was on her car, Shannon, and that fine, black muthafucka named Strong. *Damn, that nigga look good.* She was confused. She had strong feelings for Shannon, but she wasn't looking at her the same way. Her mind was running a thousand ways. Fuck it! She figured she would deal with one situation at a time.

She called her insurance company and found out she had rental coverage. She decided to still let her dad Western Union her some money. And

Enterprise Rentals was going to pick her up at five to take her to pick up the car. *One problem down.*

Then she looked at Strong's card—Triple Strong Entertainment. She wondered if she should call. She looked at Strong's number: 757-292-xxxx. *What! Seven five seven. That's the crib. He got to be from VA. That's why he was with Ant.* She dialed his number.

"What the deal?"

"Hello, Strong. This is Angela." She hoped he caught the voice.

"Champagne?"

"Yes. I prefer Angela, if I'm going to be social."

"Me too. Talk to me. What's up?"

"Just callin'."

"No, you ain't just callin'. What time we gettin' up? You at work?"

"Yeah. I go to lunch at twelve thirty."

"Where you at?"

Angela took into her own hands to give directions. "GA400 to Exit 9. Go right, second light make a left, straight down on the right. I'll be out front at twelve thirty. MCI Building," she said feeling funny inside, but hoping he said he would be out front.

"See you, cutie." Strong never gave her a chance to respond.

"Damn, he rude," she said to herself. She walked back to her desk smiling.

It took 12:30 forever to come. Angela looked in her hand mirror, checking herself. She adjusted the skirt that stopped just before her knee, smoothing out the blouse that was on the outside of her skirt, but stopped just past her stomach. Her heels gave her a walk that demanded eyes focus on her.

She walked out and glanced around. *Damn, I*

didn't even ask him what he was driving. Then she saw someone arrive. She caught a side glance and knew it was him. She walked over to the rented Cadillac.

Strong had flown in and rented a whip.

"Hello."

"What's up?" Strong said.

"Good to see you again," was Angela's response.

"So what you feelin'?" She checked Strong out. She expected jewels, foreign car, and a nigga talking about dough and his rims, trying to impress, but what she found was a laid-back, black ass nigga with Rocawear jeans, wife-beater, white T and white DC's.

"Anything. Show me your town."

"We'll go to Ruby Tuesday—and this isn't my town. I've been down here three months. Love the city, but it's not as easy to make it as people say." Angela gave him directions.

"No matter where you go, you have to work—nobody givin' away shit." Strong took in a full glance of Angela's outfit and body. "So where you from?"

"Seven-city VA. You don't know?"

Strong smirked. "Seven-city VA?" He opened the door to the restaurant.

"Yeah, the Hampton Roads consist of seven cities—VA Beach, Norfolk, Chesapeake, Portsmouth, Suffolk, Hampton, and Newport News, home of VA's, Allen *I*." Angela had been in this guy's presence for thirty minutes and she was totally relaxed. She was already feeling him. Nobody pulls her in like that.

"I heard that. So where you from in the seven cities?" Strong was enjoying every moment of this fine-ass, young shorty "reppin" VA. *A bitch from the crib. If she's a real bitch from out the way, she supposed to know how to read, figure out, and adjust to a nigga like me and pull me in.*

"You from LE?"

"Right down the street. L and J."

"I got peoples in Richmond. I've been through there going cross the Bay Bridge."

"Then you go right past where I grew up." Strong wanted to pull her in too, see what she knew. "I've been out your way to Norfolk—Norfolk and LE niggas ain't shit."

Angela looked at him. "You crazy. You won't fuck around there. Real niggas done came out of the seven cities." She was in ghetto form and didn't give a fuck. *This is me,* she thought; *I ain't frontin' no more.*

"Who? Name ten niggas from Tidewater that I heard of?" Strong had her going.

"Stacy, Speed, Donnell, Lo Max—that's Norfolk. I can go to the Beach. Goddamn, I can go to Bay-side—that's the school I graduated from—and name ten—Lee-Lee from Bayside niggas, Big Lloyd from Southgate, Pimp . . . I forgot where Pimp was from. He got along with everybody; he floated LE, Bay-side Arms, and Northridge. Everywhere."

Black's heart dropped. Pimp went to school with him. He had gotten gunned down, two tragedies that hit Bayside hard. And Boot. He kept his shit so on the low, nobody ever thought he was even hustling. She was naming everybody he knew. Her names brought him out of his daze. All the niggas from out the way who were true hustlers and got caught slipping opened his eyes and made him smarter.

"Bo, Lo. Poppa—"

"I don't know none of them niggas," he lied.

Out of nowhere she said, "I bet you heard of Black, from Lake Edward. And I know you heard of Kenny Speed. Both of them niggas ain't nobody to even fuck with," she said seriously, as if she knew.

Strong's attention was caught, but he knew she didn't know Black, and she ain't know Speed. Just heard shit just like everybody else.

An hour passed quickly. He threw the amount on the table, and they were out. He pulled in front of her job.

"I've enjoyed myself. Thanks for lunch, Strong. I didn't give you much of a chance to talk, huh! I guess I needed somebody to talk to."

"So what's your situation, Angela?"

"What you mean?"

He gave her a "be serious" look.

"Well, I'm like kind of involved. I cut it off and I'm just trying to pull it together. I don't know what I want from you, Strong. I don't know nobody here except for my friend I moved here with—I don't fuck with the girls at the club. Just get mine and I'm out."

Black began to figure he had her pegged wrong. Maybe she was trifling and about games, chilling with him and giving him that "I-got-a-friend" shit, and she didn't just live with him and she had moved from VA with him too. *What did he look like?* "Right." He looked into Angela's eye, catching her light brown eyes, then her slim neckline, straight to her cleavage, down her thick, brown legs. He had to find out what was up with her.

"You leavin' tomorrow?" she asked, not wanting to get out.

"Yeah. Why you ask?"

"I would like to see you later. You have to eat dinner, right?" Angela held her head down.

"Yes, I do." He reached out and touched her hand. "Give me a call and we'll catch up." Strong leaned with his back against the door and stared at Angela.

"Before I go, can I ask you three quick questions?"

He looked at her like it was okay.

"One—do you have a girl?"

"No."

"Two—where you from?"

"VA, Richmond."

"Three—what do you do?"

"Promote shows."

"That show the other night at 201 Courtland?"

"Yeah . . . when the artist performed. Triple Strong Entertainment, baby, we doin' it big."

"I look forward to seeing you later, Strong. Then I'm going to talk to you and really tell you about Angela, okay."

"Definitely." *She had to really be bad news for him not to fuck with her,* he thought to himself as he watched her walk into the building, dressed like a businesswoman, with the ghetto button turned off.

Strong grabbed his phone and dialed Lo.

"What the deal, cuzzo?"

"Fuck y'all niggas doin'?"

"Workin'. What else?"

"What's all that noise, nigga?—Y'all bullshittin'. Where y'all at?"

"We up here by the restaurant," Lo said.

"When Dee say we openin'?"

"They say in a week," Lo told him. "Pass me that Belvee."

"Who up there with you?"

"Poppa, Mike-Mike. Poppa gettin' ready to burst to Virginia Beach General. He just had a baby. His girl had a few problems, so she gonna be in there a few extra days. So he been hangin' over there. I'm gonna dock his pay." Lo laughed. "Kev with Dundee?"

"Dundee gone to kill somebody," Mike-Mike yelled.

"That nigga stupid." Strong laughed. Tell Poppa congrats. I got to pick something up for him.

"Lo, I met this girl here, from L and J Gardens. Her name Angela. Graduated from Bayside in '96."

"Brown skin, nice titties, real cute?"

"Yeah."

"Poppa, you know that girl Angela?" Lo asked. "Went to Hampton from L and J. Always out LE with that red bitch with grey eyes."

"Walk around like she the shit, fuckin' niggas' lives up." Poppa let Lo know he knew who she was.

"Who? Angela?" Mike-Mike sipped the Belvee out the bottle, passing it to Lo. "Tell Strong don't fuck with that bitch. Give me the phone. Heah, Strong."

"What up, Mike-Mike?" Strong knew he was about to hear a story.

"Her and her peoples be trickin'. One of these big-money niggas had a party and niggas was tryin' to trick. That one you hollerin' at all right. Only thing, she killed two niggas—I mean one nigga killed two niggas over her. Then he ended up dead."

"Who?"

"The one who shot them. She had a baby by one of the dead niggas. Her cousin was somewhere one night saying she hadn't fucked a nigga since the other one got done up and that a bitch turned her out. Say she ran to ATL chasin' that pussy-eatin'-ass ho, but you know she triflin', leavin' her baby behind some bitch eatin' her pussy—" Mike-Mike took a break from the story—"Somebody give me a black."

"Give me the phone, Buc." Lo took the phone. "Yo, I think some of that shit true, but Buc fucked up a story."

"Yeah, but that's a lot information. I just took her ass to lunch. She supposed to be hittin' a nigga later. I know she is."

"Damn right!"

"So she live with a bitch, Lo. Damn! Nigga can't be jealous over another ho." Black laughed.

"Yeah, bitch got to at least think she can get pregnant when you bust in them—that brings out that deep love." Lo stepped away from everybody. "Yo, I've been meanin' to talk with you. When you was gone, there was some cats who came in and handled shit. Say they were from Up Top. They were definitely gettin' it. They opened at a studio called Notorious Records & Notorious Tapes & CD's & Notorious Gear and they had some more shit but not 'round here.

"They came in for a minute, held it down, then they burst. They got the club on Bonny Road, Donzi's. Well, anyway, they back. They moved in

Lake Edward on both sides—families—and it's about seven or eight wild-ass niggas, and they ain't scared. But you know I don't give a damn about that. Check this—niggas talkin' like Mont and them gonna start fuckin' with them."

"I ain't worried about that."

"So . . . do I need to call Black, or can Strong handle this?" Lo laughed. " 'Cause I don't like that nigga brother anyway. Something in my pocket got his name on it." Lo felt the 9mm bullet.

"If you go, you gotta go correct. That nigga rude, Lo, but we ain't there yet. Business first. Let's see how much dough here. I'll be back to-morrow." Strong hung up and headed to Ant's house to finish his business.

"Goddamn, this shit hot," he said as he pulled into his driveway that went completely around.

Ant greeted him at the door. "Come on in."

"This shit is nice, kid."

"Yeah, this my dream. No matter how much money I make, this is me—five-bedroom, play-room over the garage, office, pool, three full baths, exercise room, three-car garage, and plenty of land. Shit, you can't get that in VA. This shit ran three hundred and seventy-five thousand. In VA Beach you know it would've cost three-quarter of a million—easy."

"No doubt."

They finished making proper arrangements. Strong was going go meet Ant's peoples in VA. Ant was going to make sure a nigga was in VA every week with twenty kilos of cocaine and two kilos of heroin.

From there Strong would put it in the streets. A lot of work and a lot of risk. But for the dough and the chance to live an elegant lifestyle, it was all going to be worth it.

"I'm headed to the other side. Gotta check this shit on the corner. This shit gettin' ready to get poppin' and we need every fuckin' dollar," Lo said.

"Don't let shit pop off over there; that shit hot enough," Poppa said, "after Dundee set shit off. Then them New York niggas be settin' out there, shootin' and playin' like it's a game."

"They'll find out soon enough. They think hustlin' in buildings was something. Wait 'til they get a taste of those LE hallways and back alleys." Lo smiled.

"Let's go, Lo. We need to get to the liquor store and catch up with Kev. I'm ready to get rollin'."

"Man, they say that X fuck you up mentally," Poppa said.

"But it make me feel good physically. I get drunk, take me two X and I'm rollin'. I don't smoke weed. I'm all right. And my hoes love when I'm rollin'. I eat up some ass, pussy, and I fucks hard. Bitch I fucked last night love me."

"That girl was a trick, Buc." Lo finished off the Belvedere.

"Why you gotta say that?" Mike-Mike was serious.

"Get the fuck in the car before you be walkin'."

"You see more when you walk, but I appreciate the ride." Mike-Mike got in the car.

Poppa understood how niggas drank, smoked, tooted, and did whatever to keep going. But being fucked up all day was beyond him. He pulled up on the other side and saw niggas at the park, standing on the corner, standing on E. Hastings, and up and down the back alley. He parked on E. Hastings.

Lo and Mike-Mike was standing outside talking. Several other youngsters had gathered because the altercation was beginning to get out of hand. Three guys stood outside of a winter-green Mercedes truck M320 with New York tags.

Poppa strolled up, intercepting some harsh words by one of the New York cats, who was trying to tell Lo they had as much right to hustle out LE as the niggas who been out here all their life.

Lo didn't argue.

"No, you don't have that right," Poppa told him. "If you trying to carve a spot, Lake Edward is not the place."

One of the cats leaning on the truck said, "Right now, all we trying to do is work the front part of LE, from Newtown on; we'll take it over later." His crew began smiling.

"Well, I ain't one to fuss and argue," Lo said. "So I'm gonna tell you for the safety of your peoples you put out here—you better stand out here with them because next time I see any niggas on these corners that don't work for us—gotta go!"

"You threatenin' us?" The New York cat stepped on the curve.

"Take it how the fuck you want." Poppa didn't give Lo a chance to answer.

"You need to calm down, playboy, and step back," one of the other New York cats said. "Come on, partner—these niggas don't know." They climbed in the truck and rolled out.

Poppa stood there as the Benz truck disappeared. "I was waitin' on you Lo, so I could tell Strong you started it."

"And I was waitin' on you," Lo said. "Shit, he told me to chill out and not to heat up the spot."

Poppa turned to all the niggas standing on the corner. "If you not out here makin' money, you need to go home. These work areas are gettin' ready to be cleared of all extras. Don't be the example."

Youngsters and non-hustlers began to move. They knew when shit was in transformation. It got crazy.

"I'm out, son. Goin' to check on my family. I'll be back later." Poppa jumped in his Suburban. "Yo, y'all, hold this shit down, and remember, if anybody comes out here makin' money, it's takin' from you," he said to Scotty and Pee-Wee.

"Actually y'all suppose to handle this corner. Don't have Dundee around this bitch wildin' out."

"Yeah! Handle your muthafuckin' corner," Mike-Mike yelled, "before I come out here and run it my goddamn self." Then he climbed in the Lex.

Lo was laughing. Scotty and Pee-Wee flipped him off.

Lo pulled in front of Precision Cuts on Baker Road. He saw the Intrepid that Dundee had rented. They were standing out front when James, the owner, came out. "Y'all got to clear my walkway." James' brother, Pop, walked right behind him.

Mike-Mike said, "Go to hell, nigga. You don't run—"

Next thing you know, James had a nice-size pocketknife to Mike-Mike's throat.

Pop put his hand around his back. "What? What?"

Everybody started laughing. Dangerous games were a part of life around the way. It was funny, but everybody knew it could get serious real fast.

Kev pulled up in his CLK430 with a shorty in the passenger side. He jumped out and joined his team. The girl walked inside the nail shop to get her nails done.

"What the deal, baby?" Kev gave everybody a pound. Then he signaled to Pop, and they climbed in the CLK and burst across the street into Lake Edward, only to return moments later.

James jumped in his 3.5 Acura, Pop followed, and they burst.

"What up, Kev?" Lo and Dundee asked.

"I thought y'all niggas were together?" Lo said.

"Naw, he wants to trick." Dundee pointed at Kev.

"Shit, I got to fuck too."

"Nigga, I'm tryin' to figure out how you pulled them niggas in," Lo said. "They movin' at least half a brick."

"Brick in half," Kev said. "Niggas know how to get it." He walked in the nail shop to check on his new, young shorty.

When he returned, Lo was telling Dundee about the disagreement with those New York cats. "They knew things were going to kick off sooner or later, but for now it was time to get this money. "I'm going across the street to the apt."

"Me too. I'll be over there in a second." Dundee wanted to hang, but he knew that wasn't his place. He was a soldier for Poppa, but if he ever got with Strong, he would become a lieutenant. Then he would gain new respect. His time was coming. He was the nigga out LE. He'd been hustlin' in Lake Edward forever, the place he was born and raised, and had to reign over niggas. He moved two kilos a week. Not Poppa, him, and it had to be recognized.

Angela walked into her apartment. She stood in the doorway, traumatized—Shannon had come in and took all of the TV's, the couch, and all of her clothes.

The thousand dollars she'd stashed in the drawer was gone. She pushed all her things off the dresser to the floor and screamed. She pressed her hands to her eyes until they hurt. *This will never happen again. Not in this lifetime, ever again.* Her hurt turned to anger.

She picked up the phone and called the front office. They were around her house in minutes, putting a new lock on the door.

She ran some bath water and called Strong.

"Hello."

"Heah, this is Angela. Are we on?"

"Of course. I'm stayin' at the Westin on Peachtree, Room 612. What time you comin'?"

"Seven thirty, eight."

"See ya."

She got out of the bath. Her body glistened from the baby oil she squirted in her bath water. She slipped into her robe and looked in the mirror.

"Angela, I'm disappointed with you. Your life is a shamble, but you from VA, bitch—you better bounce back."

She knocked on the door. He didn't answer. She knocked again. The door opened, and she walked in. She caught a glimpse of his back with BLACK across the top and REIGN at the bottom. His left tricep read ST8, and the right tricep read RAW.

He walked to the room and returned wearing Pelle Pelle powder-blue velour sweats and a wife-beater. "You early. Seven thirty or eight usually means eight thirty or nine."

"How were you going to be spending your time until I got here?" she watched his muscles flex with every movement of his arms.

"Sparkin' and getting' my head right." He picked up his Backwoods. "Want some Hennessy?"

"Sure. What you got to go with it?"

"This weed."

They both laughed.

"No. I meant soda or juice, or better yet some Alizé—the gold-colored Alizé."

"I don't need shit fuckin' up my Henny, but here is some Alizé." Strong handed her the bottle. Then he lit the Back and turned on the radio.

She sat there feeling like she wanted to tell him her life story. Being in his presence made her feel good.

He walked out of the room. When he returned he had put on his jewels—stainless Breitling and a platinum chain with a platinum cross, flooded with diamonds and hanging down to his stomach. Nothing big, but an eye-catcher.

"So what did you have to tell me? You gonna tell me about Angela from Seven-City, VA?" He smiled.

"Yes, I am going to tell you all about Angela from VA and about Angela who lives in the ATL." She let out a deep breath and began to tell Strong about Ray, Mac, Damien, and Li'l D, all the way to her best friend Rome dying so tragically. By the time she got to physically fighting Shannon, going home and her shit and money gone, her eyes watered, and the tears covered her face.

"I don't know how I got here, but I'm here. Could you begin to understand?"

Strong took in Angela's every word. He decided then that if this bitch was telling the truth, she was at a new point in her life. "Let's go out for a ride; I can put my final miles on the rented Cadillac."

"I got a rental too—they gave me a convertible Sebring."

"For real? Then you drive; you know the land, and the wind can blow in my hair." They both laughed and headed out the door.

They rode up Peachtree to Buckhead, checking out the many clubs on Pharr Road.

Inside a club called the Living Room, Angela found herself standing in front of Strong as he stood there holding his double Henny and a Heineken.

She moved like a skilled dancer.

He leaned back and enjoyed the beauty of this young girl as she seduced him. He looked around at everything and every woman going by, but they didn't matter. Strong looked at her and smiled.

"Don't you have a plane to catch in the morning?"

"Yeah, why?—Don't you have to work tomorrow?"

"Yeah, but I'm all right."

"I'm all right too," he said, his platinum glistening from the flashing lights in the club.

The deejays decided to slow it down and played a slow melody by Aaliyah.

She turned to Strong, moved closer, and stared

into his eyes. She broke the stare as his arms went up to sip the Henny he held with his left hand and secure the Heineken he had in the right. (Its purpose was really for niggas who acted up.)

She placed her body against his.

He placed his arm on her back, making sure to spill no Henny, to let her know she was secure, and they fell into a moment.

When the rugged sounds of Pastor Troy that came blasting through the speakers broke the mood, she eased back.

Out of nowhere, two guys came up. " 'Cuse me, fool," the boy said with a mouthful of gold, almost stepping between Strong and Angela.

The other guy stepped closer to Angela. "You tryin' to make that money tonight, shorty?"

Angela felt like shit. This is the shit that came with dancing, everybody thinks you fuck for money.

A feeling shot into Strong's gut. They might be saying fuck me, or are these country niggas this stupid? "Are y'all niggas really tryin' to talk to her or you tryin' me?"

Angela prayed. *Please let this guy walk away, God. Please.*

"Take it how you want, f—" Before the big guy could finish, the Heineken bottle shattered his gold teeth, splitting his lips and nose.

Angela turned and quickly slammed her glass into the other guy's head, shocking Strong.

Black grabbed Angela's hand and eased out the club as the crowd grew larger. They got to the car and got out as quickly as possible, making their way down Peachtree back to the hotel. Strong came in and poured a drink.

She went to the table and began rolling.

He removed his T-shirt and DC's then walked in the bathroom to wash his face. He returned and sat down.

She passed him the Back already rolled and lit.

He hit the L hard and then exhaled. "Next time, you get the fuck out the way."

"Shit, next time I'll know it's coming. I thought it was, but you still caught me off guard."

Angela was glad he finally spoke. It was a long ride back to the hotel in silence, and she thought it better if she just kept her mouth shut and followed his lead. "I'm sorry that happened." She held her head down.

"Heah . . . Never say sorry . . . makes you sound weak." Strong rubbed her back.

"I know you can take care of yourself, but you don't need to get caught at the club dancin'. Your rent will still get paid."

"When you comin' back to Atlanta?" she asked, resting her head on his chest.

"Now that I have a reason, real soon, cutie; real soon."

"Every reason in the world."

She put her arms around him and kissed him. She laid her head on his chest and he hugged her, and they fell into a deep sleep.

Strong arrived at Norfolk International at noon. He went and got a drink as he waited on Dee, flyin' in from Charlotte at 12:45.

Dee walked in and ordered a Henny straight.

"What the deal, son? How Chantel?"

"She good to go. Workin', studyin', doin' everything but taking care of her man. I got to damn near kill myself before she'll stop and pay some attention. She'll get me smiling, then go right back to her business."

"She just tryin' to get hers, man. She's a good girl; you know you can count on her."

"Yeah. Sometimes it takes more. So what's up with you?"

"Twenty joints and two things of diesel."

Dee reminded him, "We don't fuck with that."

"We do, and you need to connect, make some calls. You know how you do. I don't have no choice; I already got it, so it got to be moved."

"True." Dee finished his drink. "Let's get outta here. Ant's peoples suppose to be here with those thangs by three; they left Atlanta at six."

"So what you get into beside handlin' that shit with Ant?"

"Stopped at Strokers. Had to straighten a nigga and met the baddest bitch—body like Tricia with bigger titties."

"Heard that. Better watch those ATL hoes. When you goin' back?"

"In about two weeks. And she from the crib," Strong said as they made their way through the airport.

Kev approached them with his new partner. "What the deal, baby? Y'all know Pop?"

"Yeah!" Pop said.

Dee remembered James from back in the day out Norview. He was always known for getting it and keeping a top-of-the-line bitch, but his little brother was young. Now the talk was he's runnin' shit, while James ran the barbershop and other business. James was playing it smart, but Dee knew he still had a hand in the game, because there was one addiction he had to satisfy and that was getting on his knees with those dice. And Dee knew why Kev and Pop saw eye to eye—the same reason their eyes were low and red, and the smell of weed drenched their clothes.

They got to the parking lot and jumped into Pop's '97 S320 Benz sitting on 20's with TV's in the headrest. They rolled out LE to the apartment on Baker Road.

Kev took Strong to meet Ant's peoples. They picked up the whip and brought it back to the townhouse in LE with the garage.

Strong got on the phone and began making calls. He had product and was determined to move it. He met Mont, Speed, Poppa, and Lo. No sooner than it hit the garage, it hit the streets. Strong even got Speed to buy a quarter kilo of diesel to try. (Strong knew he'd be back in the next couple of days.)

Dee jumped out of the 2000 bronze-colored Yukon Denali sitting on 22's as he jumped out in front of the restaurant. "What's the deal, baby?"

The restaurant was open, and business was off the hook. At first they thought it might become a neighborhood hangout, but then Dee had the idea to advertise Moms' and Aunty's work. He went to Buda Brothers, the area's hottest radio personalities, and they pumped the restaurant across the airwaves. With commercials and neighborhood fliers, business increased. Once the website was built, and packaging and distribution began, it was unbelievable.

Dee stepped up, giving dap to his brother's team. He was cool with everybody, but Strong kept him away from all that bullshit for a reason. The only niggas that came to his spot was Kev and Lo, and that wasn't that often.

"We see who makin' all the money." Mike-Mike jumped inside the Denali. "Give me fifty dollars, Dee."

"You know I'm scramblin', nigga." Dee stepped up on the curve, letting the new navy blue Wallabees scrape the concrete.

The khaki shorts and navy-colored Sean John shirt let niggas know he wa'n' hardly scrambling. In the last month Strong had made close to a million dollars. He'd moved eighty kilos of coke and over ten kilos of heroin and wa'n' nothin' stoppin' the flow.

Dee walked inside the restaurant, leaving the truck in front running, and walked in the back getting hugs from Moms. She still hadn't seen Strong because he didn't go to her house at all.

Dee told her that the dough came from the promotional shows that were being done in ATL and Charlotte.

He seasoned four wings, floured them, dropped them in the grease. Got some fries and dropped them. He talked to his moms while his food cooked. She had aged tremendously in the last decade. Through her struggles, she continued to put God

first. Dee knew that it was through her prayers and
by the grace of God they were here. Their family
was destroyed once before, but he knew there was
no way it was going to stop. Strong was feeling secure in his system and was seeing money he hadn't
seen in a long time.

"You givin' the Lord His share of this money?"
Mom asked.

"Yes, I paid some ties," Dee said seriously.

"Stop lyin'. You ain't been to church. You need
to give the Lord at least one Sunday. It would
make me feel so good to look and see my son in
church."

Then a look of sadness came over her face.

Dee knew her thoughts went to Black and Junie.

She started mixing her potato salad to clear her
head.

Dee kissed her on her sweaty forehead, threw
his wings, fries, and scooped up some greens and
walked back out front. He was standing out front
with Kev, Lo, Mike-Mike, Poppa, Pop, and Dundee,
when Strong pulled up in his new Cadillac Escalade.
This was going to be Moms first time seeing him in
four years.

He pulled in front of the Denali. They were grill
to grill. Dee watched as the navy blue Timbs hit
the sidewalk. Maurice Malone jeans and white
T-shirt, Strong joined his team that was out front
hollering at the many females going in and out of
the restaurant, the nail shop, NY Hair Salon, or
Stellar, the beauty supply store.

The restaurant was in a prime location. Always a
view.

Strong walked over to Dee and grabbed a piece
of chicken. "Everything a'ight?"

"No doubt. Waitin' on you, kid."

"What's goin' on, Strong?" Mike-Mike said. "You goin' to put me with Monica, shorty's cousin?"

"Gotta see. They don't know who I am; they don't know I'm connected to LE, son. Know what I'm sayin'?"

"Yeah! I see what you sayin'." Mike-Mike sipped his Heineken.

"You know we don't need no shit up here—need to do something with that," Strong said.

Mike-Mike went and sat in Strong's truck. Dee and Strong looked at each other and walked inside. Lo followed.

Black peeped over the shutters. He looked at Moms. He always knew he would see her again, but he always prayed it would be while she was standing. He walked in the back.

"Heah, Ma," Black said as she stepped out.

She stopped in her tracks. A look came over her face, her eyes turned glassy, and the tears fell. She threw her arms around his neck, squeezing with all her strength.

Black held his mother. He knew she was praying and he wanted and needed her prayers.

She placed her hands on his chest and stared into his eyes for about two minutes. "So you okay?" She wiped her eyes.

"I'm all right, Ma. I'm all right."

"The police still lookin' for you."

"Naw," Black lied. But he wasn't worried about the police. His only worry was trying to duck these ruthless cats trying to take his, and the Feds.

"Stop lyin'—I wa'n' askin' you, I was tellin' you. They still come by from time to time."

"Don't worry, Momma." Black gave her another hug.

Auntie walked into the kitchen and set bags down. "What the hell—" She hugged Black. She understood her sister's happiness. They had shared the same heartaches and tragedies.

"So what you doin' in here? Ain't the police still lookin' for you? Yo' mamma said they knocked on the door the other week. Get your ass outta here and be careful."

Black walked back into the dining area, giving Dee a pound and a hug, then a pound to Lo.

"So what's up, cuzzo?" Lo asked. "You know the fifth annual Lake Edward basketball tournament is comin' up?"

"You still gettin' a squad?"

"Hell yeah! Kev playin'; him, Dre, Li'l and them niggas."

"Just makin' sure. Niggas gonna be out that bitch. New whips and all, just like a car show. Mad teams comin' from Norfolk, and them niggas across the water that fuck with Allen *I*. You know them niggas comin' with phat-ass shit.

"No doubt."

"What y'all niggas know?" Lo said going back outside.

They were standing in the front, checking bitches, hollerin' at ho's passing by, never being disrespectful because it was a place of business.

"So when do we close on those other two houses?" Strong asked.

"Next week. I know you enjoyin' your condo," Dee added.

"Who would ever think I could buy that back—

three-story with an elevator, loft and Jacuzzi, with a clear view of the Chesapeake Bay." He went deep in thought. "I go in there, Dee, and sit on the couch, roll some of that 'dro in a 'Sweet Backwoods' and I sit there and through that glass on the water, I find peace." Strong stared into nowhere.

"Better enjoy it. Paid dude thirty thousand above askin' price, that he got in cash as soon as he signed the contract. Shit, he broke his hand signin' that shit."

They all laughed.

"Know what, Dee? I been to ATL once and chilled with Angela since we met. I want to fuck with her. I want her in the ATL. But I want to bring her here, so I can really enjoy that condo."

"Do your thing, son. Nigga can feel a bitch. I know I can. So if you see her bringin' you happiness, bein' up under you, fly her ass in for the tournament. Parties, cookouts, you know the deal.

"So what you gonna do with the new shit? I can't believe you went all out. That shit is off the hook—five bedrooms, four full baths, three-car garage in Indian River Plantation. You way out there in Virginia Beach."

"That's where I can sleep. I'm gonna enjoy my shit like Scarface—by myself . . . until I find a wife."

"Don't compare yourself to that muthafucka," Dee told him.

"Naw, kid. I would of did the whole family—nobody's family matters but my own."

Dee had called Freddie Mac, a well-known realtor, once he had spoken with William L. Tyler,

CPA, his accountant for E Corp, the restaurant, and Triple Strong Entertainment. Money was being pushed through all the businesses and getting a loan was never a question. The condo Strong was in on the Chesapeake Bay, as well as the condo Dee owned, were both bought under no doc loans. Dee put down thirty percent on each property, and the bank financed the rest. No documentation whatsoever. Freddie Mac was the fucking man. Now with this new accountant, it was five percent down for any property in the US.

"We have to get a base," Strong said. "We have to get safes put where they never have to be moved. We sittin' around here with three hundred thousand in the refrigerator and another three hundred thousand in the trunk of the parked car. I'm riding around with two hundred thousand in the trunk. We need these houses. Next time we go to ATL, we buyin' cribs. I want some fly-ass shit. Spend about seven hundred thousand."

"Gotcha. You only got to tell me once." Dee smiled. He had already peeped some fly shit in the ATL.

"Vianna suppose to be closin' on a house in Alpharetta, up GA400 in North Atlanta. She found a four-bedroom, two-and-a-half bath for two hundred eighty thousand. I gave her the eighty-four hundred down. Money safe there. Tricia been lookin' at houses too. The realtor sent me some pictures through the internet. House over in Stone Mountain—four-bedroom, three full baths, and a two-car garage for one eighty, fifty-four hundred down. Let me show you." Dee reached in the truck, pulled out his laptop, and showed Strong pictures of the house.

"Find me one like that—I think Angela will like that. Then I can have a comfortable spot, and I can use her apartment for heads comin' down visitin'."

"No problem. I'll put dude on it."

"Oh, I still want some nice shit for us. Show them ATL muthafuckas how we really get down. Let me holla at Poppa. So what's up, Poppa? How's the family?"

"Not good. Girl had the baby couple days ago and something not right. They won't let her come home, so I got my other little one. Shit ain't no joke."

"Check this—front Dundee those five bricks. Get Lo, make them niggas come here and get that money. Tell him to set it up and holla back. Make sure it's in our favor . . . we talkin' about five of them thangs."

Poppa and Dundee walked over to Poppa's rental, and everybody started dispersing.

Then Dee's phone rang.

"Hello, love," Vianna said. "You busy?"

"Talkin' to my brother. What's goin'?"

"Tell him I said hello. I got the loan officer everything. They just verifyin' funds. We should be closin' at the end of July," she said with her high-pitched voice. Vianna kept going on and on about how she was going to decorate. "I'm gonna let you run. Call me later. I love you."

Soon after, Poppa called Strong to tell him Dundee's peoples were coming in the morning.

"Got some shit goin'. Gettin' ready to make moves into Carolina. It's on," Strong told Dee.

"Get it, son. I'm talkin' to this cat I know from Norfolk State. He was tellin' me how the white folks put their money into insurance companies, savings and loans, and it's secure. He was also sayin' something about trust funds, basically lettin' attorneys control your money. You makin' enough to let people handle your money making sure it's secure. Yours, the restaurant, that's over a mill a month—gotta do something to secure that."

Strong knew Dee would make sure they never ended up broke like they did before. He knew his brother was on top of every cent of this money.

Strong's phone rang, and so did Dee's. It was Tricia calling. She told him that she was a week late and was never late.

Dee had stopped using condoms with Tricia two months after they met, and for two years she never got pregnant. He thought she couldn't, even after she had a child already. *How stupid was I* Dee thought.

Strong was still on the phone. "So what's your plans when you get off?"

"The same as everyday—go home, kick back, sip on some thug passion since the thug I got a passion for isn't here. So I'll put on one of your T-shirts, spark an L, light some candles, and relax. I'm missin' you, Strong."

"So . . . I'm gonna be in VA Beach for the week-end at my beach house. You wanna fly in?"

"Yeah! When? I'm off tomorrow."

"No. You have an appointment tomorrow at ten. A real estate agent from Re/Maxx gonna pick you up, take you and show you five cribs. Choose what you like, and we'll see if we can make this happen."

She was speechless.

"Okay. So afterwards . . ."

"Yeah, soon as you finish. Take pictures, so I can see your choices." Strong smiled.

"Fuck you smilin' about?" Dee said. "Actin' all soft and shit."

"I'll call you when I get home," she said passionately and hung up.

"She comin' in?"

"Yeah. Tomorrow. You seen my niece, kid?" Strong asked Dee.

"Yeah, she doin' good, growin' the hell up. Her moms cussed me out. Told me don't come around or she was goin' to call the police."

Strong grinned at the thought of Tara wilding out. Tara was mad cool, but when it came to Dee, it was definitely a thin line between love and hate.

"She got reason to hate you, man."

"Look who talkin'."

"We talkin' about you," Strong reminded him.

"Nigga, I was young, she was young. I never had that much money. Shit, I felt the money was enough for her and my daughter. Money came, and the bitches came and never stopped. I was wrong a lot of times, but things happen in life. Fuck it—love me. Just love me," Dee said.

"She ever call you back?"

"Yeah. I just gave her a stack of fifties, two grand to be exact, and my phone number. She called like twenty minutes later. She say maybe I can get her later if she ain't got to watch her little brothers."

"What?"

"Yeah. Bitch done had two more young 'uns and still no man. I went and saw her. She look good and doin' good." Dee asked, "What about you?"

"Shereena in Florida. Married, doin' well. So I

called her moms. We gonna meet later when she get her for the holiday. And Tia, I've always stayed in touch with her. Me and Tia was close. She knew my moves before I knew them. And she knew my moves when I broke out. Somewhere along the way, she became my best friend and I'll always have love for my baby momma. Even if I'm not with her, she will never want for anything—I'm on some real shit. And believe me, her and my daughter are fine." Strong gave his brother a pound. "I'm gettin' ready to burst; I got business."

Chapter Ten

"*It's F-r-i-d-a-y and I just got paid
Ready for tomorrow to-show-my-niggas-ass . . .*"

Dundee came out of 7-Eleven singing, thinking about the twenty grand he'd just made off his peoples from Carolina.

He got in the rental, which Scotty was driving and said, "I got to go to the mall. Need some new DC's and Timbs."

Pee-Wee sat in the back smoking, not giving a fuck. "You buyin' me something?"

"Hell, naw—y'all muthafuckas makin' more money than me."

"Talk yo' as off, nigga," Pee-Wee said; "we don't hear that shit."

"Y'all make mad dough off those packages," Dundee said. "I might see two grand."

"Kill that shit, Dundee—you got us," Scotty said.

Dundee knew Scottie knew about the twenty thousand. Scotty was to Dundee like Dee was to Strong, older, with Dundee looking up to him like a big brother.

"There's Lo and Mike-Mike in front of Precision Kuts." Scotty said. "Ain't that Kev . . . comin' from Brandywine?"

"Yeah! Pull over there. See what them niggas doin' today."

"I still can't believe what them niggas did to Bo and Rome," Pee-Wee said.

"That was that nigga Strong work. Nigga rude," Dundee said. "I couldn't even look at that shit; I turned my head."

"And you want to work right with that nigga— see what happens when you cross him," Scotty said.

"I ain't gonna cross him if I get in. I just got to get Poppa out the muthafuckin' way. He gettin' my money;" Dundee pointed out. "He ain't never put in no real work."

They parked and jumped out the car.

"Where the cookout at, niggas?" Mike-Mike asked.

Dundee pulled his pants up that were almost to the ground. "That's why we came over here."

Lo laughed. "You a funny nigga."

Mike-Mike told Lo, "Tell Kev Strong said get a cookout poppin' at Bayview Park. Tell everybody out LE."

As Kev approached, Lo said, "You, Strong said get a cookout goin'."

"I ain't got no money." Kev stood in front of them in a new Phat Farm sweats and T-shirt, white DC's, and jewelry dangling.

Pop and James walked out of the barbershop.

"What y'all got on this LE cookout?" Kev asked.

"Got my lips on whatever y'all cook," James joked.

Niggas laughed.

Pop wanted to know. "When y'all doin' something?"

James threw a fifty to Kev and went back in the shop. "Let me call some hoes."

Lo called Poppa.

"Yo! Poppa said whatever in the pot he'll match it. Buy some T-Bones," Lo yelled.

In a matter of minutes, Kev was holding four hundred and fifty dollars. "Match four fifty, Poppa."

"A'ight. Carry that shit to Murray's—a thousand dollars. Tell everybody out the way. I'll check y'all when I leave the hospital. I got to pick up my other child."

Lo could tell something wasn't good. "You all right, Poppa?"

"Yeah, man, I'll be all right."

Kev picked up the phone and called Strong. "Poppa matched. We got a gee, headed to Murray's Steakhouse, discount meat market."

"Fuck you talkin' 'bout?"

"Lo said *you* said get together a cookout."

"I ain't said shit."

"You a lyin'-ass nigga, Lo." Everybody started laughing. "It's on now, nigga. Get it poppin'."

"Where y'all at?"

"Precision Kuts. Brandywine."

"Oh, where they doin' this?"

"Bayview—right, Lo?" Kev said loud so Lo could hear, but in the phone for Strong to catch.

"Tell Lo, since he lied, to spend five hundred at the liquor store." Strong's phone beeped. "Call Dee, tell him what's up, and to holla at a nigga." He clicked over to the other line. "What?"

" 'What?' Is that any way to answer the phone?"

"Naw, cutie. How are you?"

"Fine. I looked at the houses and it came down to two. Beautiful. I can't wait to show you."

"Okay, baby, I can't wait to see it."

"I got something to ask?" she said quietly.

"What?"

"Do you have anything really planned for us?"

"Just ask, don't play."

"Dream don't have anything to do over the weekend. She quit the club too after I ain't show up. She said that was her signal, but she ain't got no plans. I know she'll love VA . . . especially this weekend."

"Bring her. And I did have plans, but we'll work around that."

"You sure?"

"Yeah. Buy one-way tickets. You may need her help drive back, so I guess it worked out. Call me and let me know what time you comin' in."

"I will. I went shopping. Got a surprise for you."

"Holla soon." Strong hung up and looked at his phone to check the time. *Fuck—one o'clock; the day gettin' away.* He called Poppa. "Everything all right?"

"No doubt. Went smooth. Lo got yours; he said he'd see you. I'll check y'all niggas at the park."

Poppa checked his phone to make sure it was on vibrate. He knew he wasn't supposed to have it on in the hospital. The streets were the only thing that was going well.

His girl had his daughter a week ago and was

still in Norfolk General and they couldn't tell him nothing. And his three-year-old son was asking for Mommy every day and he didn't know what to say.

He sat down with his girl's aunt and held her hand.

Her moms walked in and gave him the dissatisfied look she'd always given him. She made no secret of her dislike for Poppa; always telling him and her daughter that she could do better.

Poppa spoke to her aunt, telling her there was no change and that he was leaving for a while.

"Go on—you look better goin'."

Poppa couldn't take it. "Your daughter up here fucked up and you still actin' the fool. Damn!" He threw his hands up.

She looked at Poppa and yelled, "You disgust me. Get out of my face—nothin'," and sat back down by her daughter's bedside.

Poppa jumped in his white Excursion. It was the Fourth of July weekend. Ballin' time—parties, cookouts, and here she was laid up. He turned up his sounds and turned on the DVD and dropped the screen. He paid the attendant and rolled out, headed to Newtown Road.

He rolled through Lake Edward. Wa'n' nobody out there, but niggas on the corner gettin' money, workers, and fiends. It was almost deserted. He turned on East Hastings.

"Yo, Poppa . . . goin' out the park?" Pee-Wee asked. He was out hustling his last few bags.

"Now that's where everybody at."

Pee-Wee jumped in the truck.

"You dirty?" Poppa asked seriously.

"Naw, nothin' but money," he said, pulling out a bundle of twenties.

They rode down East Hastings and headed out.

"That lady still got that wreath on her door."

"Hell yeah, and Dundee talkin' about killin' her because she suppose to testify against him," PeeWee said.

"Young nigga better slow down," Poppa warned.

"One on one, Poppa—he wants your spot."

"I know. Like they say, keep your enemy's close; he'll fuck up his own self. But he's a money-gettin'-ass nigga."

"You got that shit right. That's because he know niggas from everywhere. And he don't give a fuck—he'll sell to anybody, rob anybody, and kill anybody. True live wire."

"Believe me, he knows that nigga talks and acts wild, but he know who Poppa is. I was doin' bids when y'all niggas was at the park eatin' dirt."

Pee-Wee laughed.

They pulled up at the park. People were playing ball, but most were standing around listening to the radio/CD boxes being played. It was about a hundred people out, and cars were still coming.

"Not bad for short notice, huh." Lo gave Poppa pound.

"What the deal, big Poppa?" Dundee gave Poppa a pound too.

Girls started hugging Poppa, kids were running around, it was going good.

Lo saw Dee pulling up into the parking lot. He met Dee so that he would park beside him. Dee parked and got out.

"Pop your trunk, fam," Lo said to Dee, opening the back to his new wintergreen, dark-tinted Benz wagon sitting on chrome.

Dee opened the hatch as Lo tossed the trash bag in the back.

"A hundred grand. Today's deal."

"Bet. I'll take care of it. Let's see what's goin' on over here." Dee checked out the crowd. He showed love to everybody and made a drink. "Where Kev?" he asked Lo.

"He comin'. Had some shit to take care of with Pop."

Dee pulled out his phone and hit Strong. "Fuck you at?"

"I got to meet Angela. Her moms picked her up from the airport, so she spendin' some time with her child. Then she gonna get dropped off at the park. She brought a friend too."

"What she look like?"

"I don't know, but she use to dance too. I know that."

"Word, word."

"Somebody got to get her—you or Kev—I don't give a fuck!"

"I'm keepin' my options open, nigga. How long you be?"

"I'm here."

Dee turned just in time to see the Escalade rolling by, headed to the parking lot.

Strong came strolling up—black Rocawear jeans, black Timbs, and white T-shirt. When you looked around, that was all you saw—white T-shirts. LE cats had a new style, crisp white new T-shirts everyday. Even the street vendors that set up shop near hair salons, and convenience stores had white T-shirts for five dollars. It was like private school, you made your fashion statement by your jeans and shoes.

"What the deal, Strong?" niggas yelled as they

gave him dap. He walked up to Dee gave him a pound and a hug. Really to say, another day together is another great day.

"What the deal, Poppa?" somebody yelled. "Fuck up with those steaks?"

"Better eat those muthafuckin' hot dogs and hamburgers and be grateful," Dundee hollered.

People started laughing.

The nigga wanted to say, "Fuck you, Dundee," but didn't know how Dundee would take it.

"Yo, yah hoes get these kids somethin' to eat. Matter a fact, I want a picture with all these kids holding a hot dog in one hand and a hamburger in the other—I don't give a fuck how old they are." Lo started going around gathering kids.

Kev, Pop, and James had pulled up in the 3.5RL AC. When Kev saw Lo running around grabbing everybody's kids, he asked, "What the hell that fool doin'?"

"He want a picture of all these bad-ass kids from Lake Edward holdin' hot dogs," Dundee explained. I'm gonna go get some Bayside Arms kids and North Ridge kids, bring out here and get them started early.

Everybody fell out laughing. They thought about all the Lake Edward against Bayside Arms fights.

"Know what, we all used to fight LE against North Ridge, LE against Carriage Houses. "Why nobody likes us?" Scotty asked.

"That shit was just to stay in practice," Strong said. "Because what happened when we went out Green Run, First Colonial, Chesapeake or Norfolk, even if you didn't like each other, we all became Bayside niggas. And is there a stronger force?"

"Hell naw. Let niggas step out on this mutha-fuckin' block." Pee-Wee did the LE holler.

Kev, Pop, and James were standing around listening, catching up on history. Pop and James were from Norview, and Kev was from Memphis, so they could relate to the pride niggas had and were holding down their hood.

"Fuck all that fightin' shit; show some love," Mike-Mike started giving all the kids hot dogs and hamburgers for the picture as Lo lined them up.

"Shut up, Mike-Mike," Pee-Wee said, "If you put the cup down you could get something done."

"Last muthafucka who talk shit to me, they found them burnt to fuck—blacker than a mutha-fucka—with his hand on his seatbelt." Mike-Mike laughed.

No one else laughed. They just looked at him and shook their heads.

"He doesn't know what to say out his mouth," Poppa said.

"Fuck them niggas and fuck all y'all. If somebody wanna fight, come on."

Niggas looked at each other and ran a dove on him, mushing him into the ground, punching him. He jumped up mad, but what could he do.

"Who them hoes over there at the table being anti-social," Lo asked.

"They with us. They from out Norview," James said.

"Well, introduce me to something." Lo walked towards them, followed by James and Mike-Mike.

Another four girls had just got out of a Ford Explorer and two more out of an old Volvo.

"Check these bitches," Kev said. "Those four tight, but these two hoes walkin' by themselves is off the hook."

"For real. Let me get my dibs in." Pop walked over and introduced himself to Dream and Angela. Dream's body grabbed him; Angela's beauty drew him right to her.

Kev automatically eased to Dream, her shoulder-length hair gleaming. He stepped close enough to catch the scent from her hair. He could tell the shit was just done. Her short wraparound dress left her breast partially exposed and swung with the flow of her ass. "I'm Kev." He smiled his bright, white smile that bitches loved.

"I'm Dream," she said laying her perfectly man-icured hand on her breast, right where her nails met her cleavage.

"And I'm Angela." She looked at Pop with her light eyes, half-open, barely moving her glistening lips. The only bitch he knew that had that type of natural beauty was on TV.

"I saw y'all get dropped off. So if you need a ride that's my AC over there sitting on them twenties." Pop smiled, and they began smiling at his comment.

"Well, you better catch his ride 'cause my shit in the shop," Kev said as if it was a joke.

"Oh, it's in the shop, huh!" Dream said it like a line they'd heard many times before.

They all laughed.

"Actually, we're tryin' to find Strong." Angela squinted in apology.

"No problem, baby. Let me show you to him."

They headed in the direction of Strong and Dee, and Kev and Dream followed, tuned in to their own conversation.

"Thought I had found my wife," Pop said as he approached Strong to give him a pound to say no disrespect. "Your bitch is bad."

Angela hugged him and kissed him on the cheek.

"Nice to have met you," Pop said before turning to walk away.

Kev and Dream was slowly strolling up, laughing and smiling.

"Well, that's Dream over there talking to dude. And this my big brother, Dee," Strong said with a feeling of pride. "And this is my little brother, Kev." Strong gave him a pound to let him know he was on his job—somebody had to get that extra.

Kev said, "Dream, this Strong; this is their other brother, Dee."

"Nice to meet you," Dream said.

Dee stared at her pretty white teeth, beautiful lips, the side view of her dress pulling from the wide hips, allowing her ass to set out and fuck niggas up. *Too beautiful to be real. This bitch is bad.* "Goddamn!" Dee shook his head. "Whew."

The girls looked at each other.

Strong and Kev gave half smiles. They knew exactly what he meant.

"Don't act funny. Y'all better get somethin' to eat. All this shit out here—steaks over there, some still on the grill; chicken, dogs, sausages, baked beans, that shit on the table."

They heard some arguing going on at the other table.

James came walking over by Dee and Kev. "Need to get Mike-Mike, man. He over there callin' girls hoes and bitches and they ain't with it."

"Lo got him. If not, tell PeeWee," Kev said.

All of a sudden Dundee's baby momma jumped on one of Dundee's girlfriends. Niggas was on the court arguing. It was time to go.

"Y'all ridin' with me." Strong headed to the truck, and the girls followed.

"Where you want me to drop you, Kev?" Dee asked loud.

"I'm all right. I'm rollin' with Strong."

"You don't want to crowd his truck; I got plenty of room."

Everybody caught on and laughed.

Kev hugged Dream. "I ain't leavin' my baby. I ain't got no car, and I guess you stuck with me." He gave her a big smile.

She got in the truck and sat down next to Kev, closer than she had to be. "I guess I'm stuck with you."

"What the deal, cuzzo?" Lo ran to the BMW wagon with Mike-Mike by his side. "Hit niggas later," he said, and he was out with Mike-Mike hanging out the window yelling.

Dee climbed in his Yukon and picked up his phone to dial Dog, his childhood friend still stationed in New Jersey. The military was treating him good—he'd bought him a home and an Escalade. They had talked earlier and he was supposed to be coming in town. Dog had been to Charlotte twice and ATL numerous times.

Dee dialed Big gees number. Him and Big G hadn't swung out in a while.

"Hello." Big G sounded mad as always.

"What the deal, partner? What you doin'?"

"Fuckin'! I'm fuckin' and you don't disturb me because you can't find no pussy."

"Ain't nobody tryin' to fuck yo' big ass." Dee laughed. Big G was the only big pimp he knew. Other big muthafuckas got pussy, but Big G always got his share and everybody else's.

"Why you ain't come to the park, stupid?"

"Told you—I was fuckin' some ass."

"Like you couldn't come out, then go back. You on some bullshit. Holla."

Dee dialed Chantel. There was no answer. He dialed her cell, she didn't answer. He got his laptop and searched her grandmother's number in Plymouth, NC.

"Hello," the older lady's voice answered.

"Hey, grandma. Chantel there?"

"Yeah, hold on. That boy gonna hunt you down, ain't he?" She gave Chantel the phone.

"Hello. You didn't answer earlier. Did you get my message?"

"Naw, I ain't even check them shit."

"So what the deal? When you be home?"

"Next week for sure!"

"A'ight. Call me later. We headed to dinner. Bye." She hung up.

Damn, Dee thought to himself, *she was always straight and direct. No softness whatsoever*. Chantel was never soft or very affectionate, but she was dependable, smart, and true. And what he liked most of all—she gave him a sense of security to know he had a hell of a woman behind him.

Dee then dialed Vianna. There was no answer. He called her cell.

"Hello."

"What da deal?"

"Why? You here?"

"No. What difference do it make? Where the fuck you at?" Dee hated that smart-ass shit.

"I'm on my way out College Park. I'll be out that way until tomorrow; my family doin' somethin'."

"A'ight. Was that hard?"

"Yeah. You always out of town. I want my time. I'm lonely. I get tired of goin' to my family shit by myself."

"So what you sayin'? Speak up now. I told you, if you want to go your way, say something. Don't fuck around and get caught up, get fucked up."

"I didn't say all that, Dee; you just don't understand."

He could hear the trembling in her voice.

"My job is sending me to Oakland for four days for training. They are putting me up in the Wynndam out there, October twentieth to the twenty-fourth. Do I have to go by myself, or will I have some company? Don't answer now because I don't wanna hear no excuses. Please try. I'm giving you enough notice. I don't ask that much of you and—"

Dee held the phone to his side, thinking, *Yeah, yeah, yeah.* He held the phone back up to his ear, and she was still flowing.

"Yo! I'm comin'. I ridin' with you," Dee said, not talking to anybody. "I'm gonna holla back."

"Yeah," she said with attitude.

Dee hung up. He started the truck and headed out to the exclusive neighborhood of Church Point across the street from Bayview Park. Several stars lived in the same neighborhood—Teddy Riley, Bruce Smith, and many other corporate mil-

lionaires. Dee rode through and stopped in front
of his newly built home. *Life had taken a turn for the
better.* He looked around at all the beautiful homes
and wondered how many of them were purchased
through illegal funds.

His phone rang. It was Strong seeing what he
was up to. Him and Kev were at the condo chillin'.

"Let me holla at Kev."

Dee asked Kev, "You 'right, nigga?"

"Damn right. Go to the spot with the garage and
look in my room."

"Bet. I'll holla." Dee lit his Garca Vega. He
turned the truck around.

As he was pulling off, he heard someone yell,
"Dee."

He slowed down and looked around. Then he
heard it again. He looked to his left and saw the
young lady standing in the driveway of one of
the finer homes. He knew the face but not the name.
He pulled over to the girl's driveway as she made
her way to the truck.

"Heah, Dee," she said. "It's been a longtime."

"Yeah, it has," he said with a confused look to let
her know he wasn't quite sure of their connection.

"Stacy—I used to be with Maria and them when
you had those parties in your sports bar."

Dee remembered Maria, but he didn't really remember her or anything about her, just her face.

"Okay. How are you? I remember the face but
not your name."

"Yeah. I was smaller then; I was the quiet one."

"I heard that." Dee looked her up and down.
"How old are you, cutie?"

"Twenty-two."

Damn! This cutie was only sixteen or seventeen hangin'

in my shit. I was twenty-four then. "So what you been up to all this time?" Dee looked into her eyes.

Her slanted, bright eyes were dazzling. With perfectly arched eyebrows, flawless skin, and small lips, her small, white, tight-fitting shirt came down to her waist and covered the largest prettiest breasts. She moved around as if she was restless, showing off that small waist and phat ass.

"I've been doing hair for the last four years. It's been goin' well. I live over here with my grandparents. I take care of my grandmother when my granddad's on the road.

"He started Mt. Zion Baptist Church downtown on Granby Street. Now he got five churches in Richmond, Roanoke, and North Carolina. What about you?"

"I sold my sports bar, broke out to ATL, and been down there for a couple years. Gettin' ready to do a club down there, so I'm back and forth."

"That's good. Whose house—you and your girl?"

"Naw, I'm rollin' solo. And you?"

"Not attached."

Dee twisted his mouth to let her know he thought she was lying.

"I'm for real. I was with this guy for four years. Two of those years he was locked up, I was true for real. He came home and wilded out. That was a year ago and here I am."

"So you don't have friends?"

"No. Because most guys lookin' for something. And if I'm with a guy, I'm with him forever—him and him only—I don't go for anything else."

"I heard that. Stacy, it was good seein' you again. I got to get ready and run."

"When are we going to talk, Dee?" She stared into his eyes. "I enjoyed talking with you."

"Me too, cutie."

"I work every day except Sunday and Monday. I'm home after six usually, so stop by sometimes or just call." She gave him the number, and he left.

He was headed to Lake Edward when his phone rang. He looked at the phone's caller ID: 770. "Hello, baby," he said. "How are you?"

"I'm fine. Sittin' here with Kay. We goin' to put some shit on the grill tomorrow. Tonight we goin' to the KAI YAH. We smokin' a blunt now, sippin' on some apple martinis we made."

"Be careful out there tonight. You know it's the Fourth weekend—drunken muthafuckas actin' a fool."

"I know. I'll call you when I get in, okay."

Dee couldn't wait to get back to Tricia. He pictured her getting out the shower and strolling around the house in her thong before getting dressed. She never knew that drove him crazy.

Dee never meant to ever compare any of the girls he was engaged with, but the things Tricia did, no one could match. Nobody cooked, waited on him, pampered him like her. Nobody rubbed his body all the time, gave massages like her. Nobody knew how to tone down his anger when shit was in an uproar. And nobody took care of his body like Tricia. Before sex, she would ensure the dick was hard.

When making love she knew how to move, gave it to him however he wanted. She gave him sex at the drop of a dime, anytime he had the desire.

When he wasn't in the mood, she would be the aggressor until he was in the mood. And whenever that time of the month came, he was still well satisfied. Her man was always taken care of, as she would say.

"If you go anywhere else, you just a fucked-up-ass nigga . . . because I never tell you no."

He thought of Vianna and Chantel. They were financially stable, educated, and they loved him with their heart, but the only one who even had a chance of keeping him was Tricia. He couldn't help being who he was, but when it was time to fuck, he had to fuck. *The hell with being with a woman who fucks when she wanna fuck and suck dick every blue moon.* Dee had a simple theory—what one bitch won't do, another one will. That don't have shit to do with love.

Kev and Dream decided to give Strong and Angela some privacy. Kev figured getting her away from her friend improved his chances anyway. He took the S500 that was in the garage—it now had VA tags with the state seal and a slight tint—so him and Dream could drive up the coast until they reached the Atlantic Ocean.

Kev realized that the beach was an aphrodisiac. Any girl who wasn't used to the beach, like Atlanta bitches and New York bitches, it always got them. Not to mention the beach house, Escalade, and Benz.

Dream was definitely looking at Kev and Strong as a perfect picture of urban elegance.

Strong walked out of his game room holding Angela's hand. He stepped on the elevator and rose to the second floor. The candlelit room allowed them to see their silhouettes on the wall as he hugged her, stepping off the elevator. He made them drinks, and she rolled an *L.* They sat in the Jacuzzi, looking through the glass that rose from the second floor to the third, exposing a perfect view of the Chesapeake Bay.

"I lived here all my life and never knew they had shit like this, not even fifteen minutes from the crib. It's amazing. The view is perfect, so are you." Strong kissed her neck and massaged her shoulders.

The sounds of the buzzer woke Strong and Angela. Kev forgot the code and was at the gate trying to get in. Strong buzzed him in.

Angela grabbed her silk robe to cover her silk spaghetti-strap nightgown. She walked out of the room and looked out at the water. *This shit is off the hook.* She went to the loft and glanced over into the family room. "What the deal, peoples?" She leaned on the rail, looking down at Kev, Dream, and Strong. "What today's plans?"

"Tournament start at eleven; it's nine now. We play at two. It will be hot as hell by then. The tournament is two days. It should be off the hook."

"Should be," Angela said. "They have it every year, and that shit be off the rocker. Niggas come from all seven cities. It be like a car show. Real car show."

Strong and Kev looked at each other and

smiled. Kev said, "I need you to drop me at Kenny Bug Shop on Monticello, so I can pick up my whip. That nigga said he'd be done by eleven."

"Well, let me shower, because once I go out the Lakes, I ain't comin' back this way until tonight," Strong said. He went upstairs to the bedroom.

Afterwards Strong, Kev, and the girls jumped in the Benz and left. Kev was driving with Dream by his side, headed downtown. Her brown legs sticking out of her beige skirt damn near had him off the road. *What the fuck was happening?* He had enjoyed her every way possible the night before and couldn't get the black thong out of his head.

She laid her hand on his. She was definitely feeling him.

Strong leaned back, enjoying being chauffeured around.

They pulled up to The Music Shop, where they had just finished putting the TV's in the headrest. They pulled the new platinum CLK55 out of the garage. (Kev had traded his other car in and got this; the CLK320 just didn't have the power, nor was the one he looked at a drop.)

Kev looked at his whip and smiled—the new convertible CLK was going to shit on niggas— eighty thousand rolling on wheels.

Strong and the girls headed to Imperial Motors, the exclusive car lot. You could go in and request what you like and in days they would have it. Strong wanted another truck for the ATL. He knew if he got Angela a truck, then he would have transportation when he hit Atlanta. They pulled up on the lot, and Angela and Dream looked at each other and smiled.

The owner greeted Strong by name. Through Strong's team alone, the car lot had made a fortune.

Thirty minutes later, Angela was leaving the lot in her new G5 Benz truck, allowing Imperial Motors to get another eighty thousand. She was overjoyed. Most niggas allowed you to drive their shit, if they cared for you or to let other cats know you belong to them, but to just show love and buy you a whip and a crib . . . Angela was like, *Whoa*!

Strong told Angela to follow him back to the crib so she could in return drop him off. She followed him, and he returned his car and jumped in the truck. This shit was nicer than the Escalade, but he wanted the Cadillac for VA.

She pulled on Witchduck Road to a storage, and Strong got out.

Angela asked him, "You gonna be a'ight?"

"For sure. What time is it?"

"Eleven. That Triple Strong Entertainment is you?" Dream asked.

"Yeah, I sponsor them. My cousin Lo got a team too for the restaurant. I'll meet y'all out at the courts in a couple hours. Kev and them definitely goin' to win the first round. Probably play again about four."

"That's good. We goin' to run to McArthur Mall and pick up a few things," Angela told him. "Need anything?"

"No, I'm all right."

"What's your size anyway?"

"Thirty-eight waist, thirty length and triple *X* shirts. Size eight-and-a-half Timbs and DC's."

"Gotcha."

Strong began to walk away.

"Heah, give me a kiss, nigga. You buy me houses, cars, clothes, but I catch hell gettin' a kiss."

Angela and Dream laughed.

Strong leaned down and gave her a kiss, and she pulled off smiling.

Angela picked up her phone. "I don't know why my girl ain't called me. Let me try this bitch again."

"If she truly your girl," Dream said, "she'll call you."

After picking up a few things at McArthur Mall they went by Angela's moms to change before going to the courts. On her way down Baker Road she saw some of her old Bayside team hanging out at 7-Eleven and pulled over. She hadn't had a chance to talk to Fat Joe or Quan since she'd seen them at Rome's and Ski's funeral.

They didn't know who she was when she first pulled up.

She got out the truck.

"Goddamn, girl. What the hell!" Fat Joe said. "I guess the ATL treating you good or that bitch treatin' you good."

"I ain't fuckin' with her no more—I got a man, son." Angela gave him a pound like a nigga.

"Heah, Quan." Angela hugged him as he approached. She smelled a certain stench. She looked at Quan up and down. His Timbs were dirty as if they'd been through three winters, three summers, and were on their way into winter number four. His jeans looked as if they could stand on their own and his once-white-turned-beige T-shirt was hanging like he had it on for days.

"What's up, Angela?" Quan barely lifted his head.

She touched his cheek and looked in his eyes. She could tell he was looking for more than weed. She looked over at Fat Joe with disgust in her eyes.

Fat Joe signaled for her to walk with him. He wasn't with Quan, but had seen him up there just like her.

Dream got out the truck and walked in the store. She came out with two cranberry juices. She was so fine, Joe stopped and Quan lifted his head. Some other cats were trying to holler, but she paid them no attention.

"So what's goin' on, Joe?"

"Not a whole lot." Joe stepped over to his Durango and grabbed a small package out the door compartment. He took two toots and shook his head, then handed it to Angela.

She took two toots and handed it to Dream in the truck. Dream finished it off.

"How Quan get fucked all up, Joe?"

"Fuckin' with them niggas on the other side. You know all I do and ever done is smoke and toot this here." He showed her another bag. "But niggas out here is losin' they minds—tootin' coke, heroin, takin' X, and puttin' crack in weed. That's what got him."

"I hate to see my nigga like that," Angela said.

"They say your girl doin' the same thing, but she ain't gone yet. Monica still lookin' good, but she tootin' probably over seven, eight grams a day."

"For real! I been callin' her since I came in yesterday and she ain't answer or call me back. How she supportin' that habit?"

"This was the part of the conversation I didn't want to have—she fuckin' with your boy Ray."

Angela's head snapped back to attention. "What?"

"Yeah, Ray started hustlin' and blew. You know he soft, so he had to fuck with those Carriage House niggas. Somehow he got dough, found a connect, and got those niggas scorin' from him. He movin' weight and Monica right there."

Angela laughed. "Not Ray."

"Oh yeah, your cousin—the bitch you was stayin' with before you left—was around here talkin' shit on you, talkin' 'bout she help shorty turn you out and how she was carryin' you to Atlanta to work."

"My cousin's a stupid bitch. I left here on a good note, but that ain't my first time hearin' that shit. I'm gonna see her soon."

"You goin' to the courts?" he asked getting in his truck.

"Yeah, I'm behind you."

"Sorry, girl, my nigga was just catchin' me up. Seem like my girl fuckin' with my high-school love and she probably ashamed—I don't want that gay-ass muthafucka."

Quan walked up to the truck. "Can I hold some-thin', Monica?—I mean, Angela."

She handed him thirty dollars. "Quan, please get your shit together. We all make mistakes and choose the wrong paths, but we can bounce back."

"I'm tryin', An. I'm tryin'."

They pulled up by the courts. It was so packed, you had to park several blocks away. Angela couldn't see it and drove closer to the crowd.

"Damn, niggas gettin' it around this bitch," Dream said.

"Niggas goin' to jail around this bitch—that's what they doin'," Angela told her. "Let me break this shit down for you. See over there"—Angela pointed to a group of niggas sitting and parked by the apartments behind the picnic tables by the courts, the Bentley's, 600 Benz—"that's Allen Iverson peoples. They come from across the water, Hampton and Newport News; they are truly rich and got backin'. They ain't about no trouble, just hollerin'.

"See those guys over there with the Escalade, Yukon Denali, and those little BMW's and the Lexus—those cats from Portsmouth and the Beach— they run with Timberland and Farrell. They got money, some of them, but they in the industry so you know."

They both said soft at the same time, "Fuck 'em!"

"Now over there, the clique with the 4Runner, Yukon, Q45, Tahoe—them niggas hustle out Carriage House. They got money and they chill-ass niggas. Love to have a good time, but they get rowdy and rude at times. Now over there in the parking lot where the black Lexus is sitting, black Avalon, white Mountaineer, Porsche—those cats from Bayside Arms and Northridge right down the street. We go to school with them."

"And those LE niggas over there where my baby CLK sittin'?" Dream asked. "Look at his fine ass. Don't even know it's us. Pull over there. They got four cones over there; maybe you can get a space."

Angela pulled up by a cone. Kev noticed her and moved the cone behind Poppa's Suburban. All eyes were on the G5 truck as the girls stepped out.

As soon as Angela's Dolce and Gabbana sandals hit the pavement, she noticed Monica. The black Dolce and Gabbana shorts hugged her hips and flowed with her movement as if they were painted on.

"Shinin', ain't you, girl?" Kev said to Angela.

She looked at him through her D&G glasses. "Like the muthafuckin' sun, nigga," Angela told him. She knew eyes were on her.

Some were her peers. They knew Angela, but they didn't know her like this.

Angela saw Monica across the court sitting on the CL600 "drop" being driven by Ray, staring his ass off from the time the G5 truck pulled up.

Monica saw her talking to Kev. She thought her truck was nice but didn't consider Kev to be any competition. He wasn't large as Ray and Ray had money now. Kev wasn't from VA and she didn't know him, but she knew he drove that platinum CLK.

"Give me a hug," Kev said to Dream, sitting in the truck; "need some good luck. We barely won that last game."

Out of nowhere you heard the roar of motorcycles, and all eyes went to the ZX9R Kawasaki hanging in the air down Newtown Road with an airbrushed picture of Junie on both sides with RIP. The rider was draped in royal blue and black, with a silver half helmet. Behind him was Lo and Pop on the Suzuki 1200 and Ducati 900ss, chromed from front to back like the other two, with loud Muzzy pipes.

Dee pulled up and jumped off the bike. Niggas gathered around checking out the paint job, some asking who Junie was.

"That was y'all's older brother?" Angela asked.

"Yeah," Dee told her. The pain of Junie's loss hit him again. He looked around and went over and hit the blunt that Pee-Wee had.

Angela looked over at Ray. By this time, Monica had made her way closer to the end, near Angela.

Angela knew that bitch wanted to talk.

"Here come Poppa. Move the other cone."

Poppa pulled up, shining in the convertible Cadillac, El Dog. He jumped out wearing a wife-beater, showing off his tats, jeans sagging, and Timbs.

"Fuck goin' on, my niggas?" Mike-Mike yelled, jumping out the Suburban with the Grey Goose.

"Put that shit up, Mike-Mike," Lo said. "Ain't no police out here. They at the restaurant eating; all of them."

Everybody laughed as he continued to take the Goose to the gut.

"Pass it here then, son."

"Who gonna win the car show?" Scotty asked.

"I already see who won that shit," Poppa said. "That hot-ass Bentley drop—rich-ass niggas. Nobody can fuck with that athlete money. Then strong second is between Kev and Ray, big ballers."

"Shit, Ray ain't no baller—his dad died and left him that business. He ain't want it, so his dad partner bought him out—three hundred fifty thousand," Mike-Mike said.

"Well, the nigga got weight and be gettin' it. If he had a quarter mill then, he might have a million now," Kev said.

"Cats say he soft, but nobody really fucks with him."

"Shit, his ass done got robbed a couple times. I know." Lo said it like he was the one that did it.

"Yeah, but two cats dead and one dismembered," Mike-Mike added. "They lookin' for the other one."

"They ain't lookin' for the other one," Lo said. "I ain't use no mask—fuck him and his muthafuckin' team."

Poppa looked at Lo.

"Ray is a punk-ass nigga, but he gettin' it and nobody fucks with him because of his cousin, Speed. Speed that nigga first cousin."

Those who knew who Speed was stared at each other and then at Lo. Everybody knew Lo was a wild nigga, but he wa'n' ready to fuck with Speed.

Out of nowhere, a black Dodge Viper and royal blue Corvette ZR1 came flying down Newtown, past the courts, doing about a hundred.

Everybody stopped and looked except for the cats playing ball.

The tinted-out Viper and ZR1 pulled up in front of Poppa, and the tinted window came down. It was Javonne, that neighborhood cat that hustled alone, light-skinned nigga with three golds in the top row of his mouth. Rocked dreads, twists, whatever you called them, with a headband around his head, pulling them back. He skidded off, racing down Lake Edward Drive.

"Fool gettin' that money, hustlin'-ass LE nigga," Poppa said.

"That's my peoples, but he ain't never put me on. He a'ight though," Dundee said.

"We good, nigga." Poppa gave him a pound.

Angela noticed Monica talking to Fat Joe. He

went to school with most of these niggas and had no beef. Angela walked across the street. "Watch my girl, Kev." She looked at Dream.

"Nobody wanna fuck with this Memphis bitch," Dream said.

"I thought you from Atlanta," Kev said.

"I live there now, but originally from Millington."

Just then, the co-ordinator got on the loud speaker and announced the next game.

"I gotta run. Don't let nothin' happen to my girl, Poppa—that's my future." Out of all the girls he'd been through, this shorty was on. He fucked around and took the condom off just the night before and that shit was incredible.

"Don't play, Kev. Goin' home the right way is a dream for Dream." They smiled.

Kev noticed Dundee and Javonne trying to park where the cones were. He yelled, "Move the cones, Pee-Wee."

Angela walked up to Monica and Fat Joe. They looked each other up and down. Angela noticed Monica was dressed head to toe in Burberry shorts, bikini top, showing her pierced belly button and banging-ass body. Her Burberry hat complimented her lightly tinted three-hundred dollar Burberry shades that covered her grey eyes. They both knew they were tight.

"So you can't answer my shit because you fuckin' with that bum-ass nigga"—Angela pointed at Ray—"and scared to be a woman and say that."

"I knew you'd act like this and I ain't got time . . . nor do I want to hear any bullshit about how I handle mine."

"Monica, I know Ray fake and you coachin' him.

He playin' what he thinks is a game and if he knew shit about it, he would know it's far from a game. And I know you—if he go broke tomorrow, you out."

"I learned from the best. My old roommate taught me to get it all at any cost," Monica said, hiding behind the three-hundred dollar shades.

"That was low. You ain't shit. You always held me responsible, but I'm livin' with that shit, Monica."

"I know you are, An. I know. Look, I know you don't want him, and if I don't drain him, some other bitch will." Monica held her hands up. "I thought you forgot the game—fuckin' with dirty-ass bitches."

"That's my past, girl. My past."

"So who you fuckin' with, girl? Kev?"

Kev had been in town a short time but had made his mark as a pretty boy with braids. Him and Pop were getting it, and they were running through some hoes.

SCURRRRRRRRRRRRRRRRRRRRRRRRRRR!!!!! was all you heard. Then the streak of bright yellow flew by, getting the attention of every living soul. The bright-yellow Lamborghini came to a sudden stop. The driver made a doughnut, and smoke clouded everybody's sight. Then he took off, beaming toward Poppa.

The car had everyone's attention, until a streak of silver flew by doing one hundred twenty miles per hour, and stopped on a dime. The driver threw the Ferrari GT in reverse. He was going backwards at about sixty and came to a dead stop.

Then the driver punched it, and the car did doughnuts in a perfect circle until it looked like a compact platinum bullet. He burst towards Dee and Poppa and stopped, then burned rubber, sitting still for about fifteen seconds.

When the smoke cleared, Ant jumped out the Lamborghini as the doors went up, and Strong got out the Ferrari.

Strong approached Dee and Poppa while Kev, Lo, Dundee, Pop, and JaVonne all crowded around the Ferrari. Ant walked over to the cats with the Bentleys and 600's.

"That shit nice," Poppa said. "Doors open like a spaceship—off the fuckin' hook."

"The nigga shit is hot," Dee said. "I like silver and the way that shit look; but the bright yellow screamin'."

"What them shits cost?" Poppa asked.

"Ferrari, two-hundred and thirty thousand, and the Lambo was fifty more."

"For a goddamn toy." Poppa shook his head.

"You can get out the truck, girl. You a'ight out here," Strong said to Dream.

She was getting ready to get out anyway because Angela had called her. She stepped out the truck. Strong couldn't help looking as she stepped to the sidewalk.

He saw the most blessed ass and hips, low-cut jeans with a bikini string going into her ass. Her tight half-shirt covering those firm 36D's that were trying to come out of the bra and free themselves.

Many girls were hating, not because of the outfit, but the body was a dream. She walked across the street, catching every eye, including even Monica's.

"So you and Kev kickin' it?" Monica asked Angela after all the commotion died down.

"Naw, girl. I fuck with his brother Strong, the guy with the white Iverson jersey and the two long platinum chains."

Monica stared and couldn't believe what she was seeing. The braids he had when she knew of him were gone. "Who Black?"

"Who? Hell naw. I said Strong, the one driving the silver sports car."

"Angela, what you say? You fuck with him?"

"Yeah, he bought that truck, girl, and we got a house."

"Girl, that is Black. The guy beside him is Dee, and the one with the dreads is Lo. Remember I told you about them a while back."

"Yeah, but I thought—" Angela got quiet as Dream approached.

"Dream, this is Monica, Monica, Dream," Angela said, not really giving a fuck.

She looked over at Black, known as Strong to her. She now understood why she was drawn to this guy—they were from the same place. She knew he had his reasons for hiding his identity, but her feelings hadn't changed. Her eyes caught his. He stared at her, and she blew a kiss.

Black gave a half smile as Monica and Dream looked on.

Dream looked over at Strong. "She got a nigga there."

"You ain't lyin'. You ain't lyin'." Monica looked over at Black.

Black stepped back on the curve as the bright yellow Hummer pulled on the grass up by where Black Russian Entertainment was setting up.

Mont and Grip jumped out with some wild-looking nigga hopping out the back—half his head was braided, and the other half was all over his head. Tall, thick, dirty-looking cat, looking like he just got off work. They walked over to Black, showing love as many did.

The directors called for the next game. It was a squad from the Lakes that Lo was sponsoring and the other squad was sponsored by Mont and those Carriage House cats, which consisted of young ballers that came to play.

"What the deal, Lo?" Mont asked. "How much faith you got in your team?"

"Holla, nigga—don't play." Lo watched as Ray whispered in Grip's ear.

"Thousand a man," Grip yelled.

Lo thought about five grand. He knew Kev, Little, and them cats were unbeatable and he had five thou, but not to lose. But he couldn't be made to look small; he'd rather go broke first. "Sound good."

Everybody moved closer as the guys stepped to the court.

"Wanna up it, Lo—ten a man?" Mont asked.

Lo looked over at Kev, who'd overheard the bet. "Hell yeah," Kev said, "I got twenty-five."

Angela and Dream came and stood by Strong, Dee, Lo, and Poppa as they watched Kev ball.

"We got another fifty over here," a nigga yelled across the court from the Carriage House side.

The score was about even and it was the third quarter. "Stop fuckin' with that nigga, Lo—bet it up; I got you," Strong said.

Angela and Dream looked at each other, eyes wide. Angela looked across at Monica leaning on Ray. She knew at that moment her and her girl had the two biggest ghetto celebrities there were, and it felt good.

"Twenty-five a nigga. Let's keep it simple. What?" Lo yelled.

All eyes fell on Mont and Ray. Mont looked at Ray and, after a couple-seconds stare, turned and said, "Bet."

It was on. These cats ran until they bled from the concrete scrapes and 'bows thrown throughout this game—if that's what you want to call it.

"Get them niggas, Kev," Dundee yelled when Kev hit three.

"Show a muthafucka something," Mont yelled.

"Here it go, here it go . . . aaahhhhhh!!!!!!" Mike-Mike yelled as Li'l slammed that shit and damn near broke the goal."

"Play that ball. Fuck 'em," Rell yelled.

"LE niggas ain't shit." Ray laughed—alone.

Those who overheard got quiet and stared.

Mont and Ray ended up winning by a jumpshot. The tournament was over for the day.

"Can I get that?" Ray hugged Monica.

"You won, but you lost in character. You disrespected LE, so you forfeited your rights to *your* money," Mike-Mike told him. "That's the rule—never disrespect the Lakes, muthafucka. You must of lost your goddamn mind."

"Fuck all that," Ray said. "Y'all muthafuckas playin' and I'm more serious than a muthafucka."

"Comin' out your mouth like that—how serious are you?" Lo picked up the basketball and slammed it into Ray's face. "Carry yo' bitch ass—I ain't givin' you shit."

"Your card has been pulled my nigga," Mike-Mike said.

Kev was still upset about losing and was acting a little hostile. "Let's burst, Lo. Fuck these niggas."

"Fuck you, pretty muthafucka—don't make me tongue-kiss your ass out here," Mont said.

Kev looked at this big muthafucka. His split-second hesitation allowed that wild-lookin' cat to come from nowhere with a broken bottle and slam it into the left side of Kev's face. Blood splattered as he rushed Kev, tackling him to the ground, and raising his hand to stab him again.

Shit happen so fast.

Lo kicked the nigga in his chest and knocked him off Kev, reaching in his waist for the nine. His hand was stopped by the hold that Grip had on his hand, and his other around his throat, forcing him backwards, trying to push Lo to the ground. But the right blow that Poppa delivered to his ear took all the strength out his ass as he dropped to his knees.

In one smooth swoop Mont made his move on Poppa, who grabbed his neck with both hands and, with his own momentum, took Mont off his feet and slammed him on top of the CL600, leaving his bodyprint.

Ray grabbed Poppa around his arms and locked his, as the wild-ass nigga jumped back up, and all Poppa saw was this crazy-looking guy with half his head braided and the other out coming at him with the same broken glass. Ray had Poppa's arms stuck.

Poppa twisted his body and turned his head, anticipating what was about to happen. In the split second, he heard the words, "Hail Mary, look at me now—"

Pow!!! *Pow*!!!!!

Ray's grip quickly came loose just in time to see the wild-ass nigga's body drop beside Kev, leaning on the table under the shelter. The cut was wide open from the jagged bottle, and he had lost a lot of blood.

Dundee pointed the gun at Ray as he dove towards his car.

Pow!!! *Pow*!!! *Pow*!!!

One bullet grazed Ray's left arm.

Black had made his way back across the street from talking to JaVonne once the commotion started. "Get him to Bayside."

The girls were frantic. Dream was upset as if Kev was really her man.

Angela sped off towards Bayside with Dream, Kev, and Mike-Mike. The police sirens got closer real fast.

Mont grabbed Grip. "Nigga, you got two strikes, and I'm on paper—we got to go. Sorry!" Mont and Grip jumped in the Hummer.

All cars were skidding out as the police hit the Lakes.

Black knew he had to go and quick. He couldn't get caught out there. He looked at Dee. Dee knew the deal and threw him the bike keys as he caught the keys to the Ferrari, parked with the Lamborghini away from the ruckus over by all those rich niggas and entertainment cats.

Dee glanced around as he walked to the Ferrari. Black's whole team was gone. He was talking to Stacy and she had disappeared right when the conversation was heating up before the gunshots. He'd told her she was going to leave with him, if she wanted his company. He climbed in the car and pulled off. He had to get to Bayside and check on Kev.

Suddenly Stacy stepped up. "You made a promise."

"I got to go to Bayside; it's on you."

She jumped in.

He smirked as he eased away from the scene of the crime.

By the time they arrived at Bayside, the whole clique was there, except Black and Dundee. Kev had to have thirty-two stitches and was granted a lifelong scar. They decided to keep him because he had lost a lot of blood. Kev was out of it—they were pumping blood into his body and had tubes up his nose. That wild nigga had got him good.

Poppa, Lo, Mike-Mike, Angela, Dream and Stacy had all walked back out to the emergency room parking lot.

Moments later, Dee came out with a sad look. "What the fuck happen? I was standing there talking to shorty and all of a sudden, all hell broke loose."

"Shit happened so damn fast," Mike-Mike said. "But it was Lo fault—he started it."

"Shut the fuck up, Buc—ain't nobody with that shit tonight." Lo looked at Pee-Wee and Scotty, who had just pulled up in Scotty's girl's car.

"Fuck . . . you can't beat my ass," Mike-Mike said. "You should of fucked up them niggas instead of letting that nigga snatch your ass up."

Lo grabbed Mike-Mike. Mike-Mike grabbed him back, and they started tussling in the parking lot.

"Chill out, man," Scotty said. "Y'all niggas still

actin' the fuck up and Kev in that bitch fucked up. That shit wa'n' suppose to happen."

"Heah—" Pee-Wee looked at Stacy—"I know you."

"Dog." Stacy remembered him from one of the young hustlers out the Lakes that Pee-Wee used to fuck with.

"Yeah, a'ight. How you been?" Pee-Wee looked at her as she stood by the Ferrari. He looked at Dee with a wicked smile and shook his knotty head up and down as if to say, "You got one, son."

Dee's phone rang.

"What's poppin'?" Black asked. "How Kev?"

"He a'ight. He got mad stitches in his head and they keepin' him overnight for observation. He lost mad blood."

"Okay. Where Poppa and them?—they ain't answerin' their phone."

"You know you got to turn shit off in the hospital. Everybody out here."

"Tell them to get to the house on West Hastings. Come through the back way through Norfolk—it's hot as hell out there. Tell Lo his bike out here. Pop went back up there and got it; both of them in the back. Where the CLK?"

"Lo got it here. Him and Mike-Mike fightin'."

"Tell them niggas I said get around here."

"Yo, Strong said he at the spot on the Hastings and y'all need to get round there," Dee said to Poppa and Lo.

"Angela and her girl still there?" Black asked.

"Yeah. Got to clean the back up; some blood got on her seats."

"Tell her to clean that shit up. She'll be a'ight. Fuck that truck—long as Kev a'ight. Fuck, I got to call his peoples; he ain't suppose to be here." Black said he knew his conversation with Polite wasn't going to be pleasant. "So what you goin' to do?"

"Ride for a second. I'll holla later," Dee told him.

"I need you to go with shorty and make sure they clean her shit out good. Pay somebody or take it up by Military Circle to the car wash."

"Man! Shit, I don't feel like doin' all that shit."

"Then tell her to hit me," Black said and hung up.

Dee showed her where the car wash was and hit them off lovely to just clean it up and not to ask a thousand questions.

After a thorough cleaning inside and out, the Benz truck was like new, and the girls were on their way. They were leaving Sunday, and Angela was ready to finish enjoying her weekend. But Dream wasn't feeling VA no more.

Before they left the parking lot, Dream pulled up beside Dee in the whip.

"Dee, Dream wants to stay at the hospital and sit with Kev."

"Go ahead. Leave her here; he'll love that. Make him feel better."

Dee smiled. *Go take care of my little brother*, he thought, saying thanks to God again as he remembered the doctor's words, "A few more minutes and he'd been gone."

Dee punched it, headed for Interstate 64. He wanted to chill with Stacy for a few before heading to the club.

They raced up and down the highway, kicking and enjoying the exotic sports car. After a long and intense conversation, he dropped her off and headed home to get right for the club. Her conversation was nice, and she made it clear that she wanted a relationship, she wasn't just giving her body up for fun. So he decided to catch her another time.

He hit Strong. They were still out LE.

"What the deal, son?"

"Gettin' my head right, sitting here. Just popped two of those 'jumpoffs,' sippin' Henny with the Backwoods burnin'. Nigga is ready for the club. Goin' to Donzi's?"

"I don't know. Tryin' to figure out all this bullshit. Niggas beefin' gonna fuck up money. Hold on, my phone beepin'." Black looked at the caller ID. "That's Mont—let me call you back."

"What's the deal, Strong?" Mont asked. "Callin' to make sure we still in business." He knew the importance of a connect. He could score from Ray, but his prices were nowhere near Strong's. And his cousin was scared of him just like many other niggas in Tidewater. Felt he'd never get his paper. But Speed still held him down.

"That young nigga was one my brother soldiers. He hot as hell about everything, but you always dealt with me."

"Yeah, we still good. Couple changes, but I'll put you on to them next week."

"A'ight, one other thing—that one fifty."

"Who you make your bet with?" Strong asked.

"You know that's your peoples, so I thought it was—"

"Again, Mont, who'd you make your bet with?"

"Lo."

"A'ight, that's who you see."

"Tell him to call me; I don't got his number."

"One," Strong said and hung up. Then he told Lo to call him, so he didn't feel like Lo was ducking him.

"What you need, kid?" Lo asked Mont when he answered the phone.

"You know what I'm lookin' for, son—don't play."

"First of all, I made the bet with Ray, and I ain't payin' him shit. And I really ain't payin' you shit."

"Who you think you fuckin' with? The last nigga to fuck with me I—"

"Naw, nigga. *I* was the last nigga, and you ain't shit in my book. Now this shit is done." Lo hung up the phone.

Black was standing there. "That was one of Grip soldiers that Dundee killed," Strong said to Poppa with a stern look. "He's lookin' for payback and Mont lookin' for his dough."

"Nobody gives a fuck," Lo said. "He was gonna take Poppa's life—it was his or Poppa's. Fuck him."

"I'm with Lo," Poppa added. "They set it off, and that nigga paid for what he started. Fuck that dead muthafucka," he said, answering his phone. He stared at the number for a second till he remembered it was the hospital. He took a deep breath and answered. "Yeah!"

"Hello, Poppa, this is Auntie. You need to get down here. Princess has taken a turn for the worse. It looks real bad, Poppa."

She heard the silence in the phone, then a low, "I'm on the way." Poppa wasn't going to accept that. *Princess ain't goin' anywhere.* They had two kids together and she'd been his rock before he did his bid. She was there when he came home, waiting with open arms.

Princess always fussed about him being in the streets; she always felt he could do better. But this was all he really knew, and this shit was making them mortgage payments, day care payments, feeding her and those kids, and was going to open his studio he had in the works that him and Dee had discussed. Princess was going to be so proud that he had a business.

"Yo, I got to run—it's Princess; she's not good." Poppa headed for the door.

"Give me a call, Poppa," Strong said.

"Let us know what's up, fam. One!" Lo added.

Dundee sat for a second talking to Lo and Strong. He was tired of paying dues, but moving up constantly. "I'm out. I'm gonna ride by Virginia Beach General and check on Poppa," Dundee said. "I got to make sure he a'ight. He quiet, but he will snap—like his ass did earlier; dude got dropped with a one-piece."

Lo hyped the story. "Naw, check this, Strong—I'm 5' 10", so I know Poppa about 5' 11", Grip 6' 2", Mont about 6' 1". Poppa had Mont off the ground and slammed his ass through the god-damn hood."

"Strong as a bitch. Mont big boy," Strong said. "Go check on my nigga, let us know. I was goin' to Donzi's, but I'm goin' to chill."

Strong hit Angela. "Heah, baby," she answered.

"Where you?"

"Gettin' ready to catch up with some friends and go to Donzi's. Why? What's up?"

"I'm headed to the condo, sit back look at DVD's."

The phone was silent. Neither was saying a word. She knew by the silence he was waiting for her response. "I'll meet you there in twenty minutes."

"Twenty minutes," he said and hung up.

"The club better not be that important. Give up those keys, Lo dog," Strong said.

"Damn! Thought I had the Benz tonight," Lo said.

"Get your bike, go home, and get your own shit. I ain't drove no CLK 55 before," Strong said as if it was a big thing. He headed to the condo and dialed Dee.

Dee was headed to Donzi's already. "What's up, son? You on your way?"

"Naw, I'm goin' in. Look, tomorrow or Monday I need you to get me three hoopties that run real good—old Honda, Lumina, Delta or some shit. I got a new set up that gonna make me sleep better. I need this done Monday."

"Bet. I'll holla," Dee said hanging up. The Ecstasy had kicked in, and he was smoking his second Backwoods to the head of this new shit called "Sour Diesel," which had him in rare form. His body was feeling great, and all he wanted was to get around some of the finest bitches in VA. It was great to be home; he was rolling, and he was ready.

Dee pulled to the front door of the club and stepped out the Ferrari as the doors went up. The line was down the sidewalk, so eyes were on the exotic piece of machinery, waiting to see who was driving.

They watched as the four-hundred-and-ten-dollar crocodile-embossed sandals hit the concrete, neatly covered by a khaki-colored linen set. Dee scanned his surroundings through the gold-and-wood, tinted Ralph Lauren glasses. His four-thousand-dollar hexagon link bracelet filled with 4ct set in platinum and ten-thousand-dollar platinum watch with the diamond bezel let lookers know he was for real.

Security stepped up. "Can't park here, player."

"Valet park that shit."

"No, you can't park here—I don't care about your money."

Dee already knew he had a hater trying to show out for the crowd like he showed nobody favoritism. "Call Youngblood." Youngblood was head of the security force and also was married to Dee's and Black's first cousin, Janielle.

"Tell 'im Dee out here. Sorry he missed the restaurant, but I hope my sister got his plate to him. Tell 'im that."

Moments later, several security was showing him love: parking the whip, and escorting him in with no pat-down, no charge, as if he was the star performing that night.

Youngblood stood talking with Dee for about five minutes with two other security cats around Dee. Youngblood introduced Dee as his brother-in-law. Each time Dee shook the hand of security, he palmed a fifty. They assured him he would never have that problem again.

Dee headed upstairs to the bar, greeting many guys and girls from years back, new ballers, same hoes and definitely new young hoes that were not playing. Dee walked to the crowded bar. He saw three young ladies ordering their drinks. He checked their style. They looked nice, but ordinary. He continued to listen to deejay Devastator rip shit like he always done.

Suddenly a gleam of light caught the corner of Dee's eye. He glanced down at the ring. She was wearing that big-ass diamond on the left hand, letting every nigga know she was spoken for. The diamond tennis bracelet and diamond earrings, the short Chanel skirt, Chanel top, and Chanel opentoed sandals with her toes beautifully pedicured with a mixture of colors, let every nigga know she was being well taken care of. She stood eye to eye with him (he'd always preferred a shorter woman). She stood talking with her friend who was dressed nice, but not with the same class and taste.

Dee walked to the bar and walked close to her, almost on her hip, crowding her personal space.

"Please order me a double Hennessy straight and a Corona." Dee threw his left hand on the bar, getting closer, where people looking on might think she was with him, making sure she got a glance of the Christian Dior watch with the diamond bezel.

She turned, moving away with attitude across her face. She glanced at the watch, the bracelet, the linen, the crocodile sandals, and then her eyes went straight to the slightly tinted Polo's, and in one quick motion returned to her original position, slightly closer with a slight smile on her face. In her nose sat the tantalizing smell of the Burberry cologne.

"I need a Hennessy straight, double and a Corona with lime," she said to the bartender. "That's all you want?" she turned and asked Dee.

"Naw, that's not all, but we'll have to find time

and talk about that." Dee looked into her eyes. He pulled a small stack of fifties, peeled off one, and handed it to her, got his drinks, and took a step back.

"Here's your change," she said, tapping Dee.

Dee waved his hand. "Did you get yours and tip her?"

"Yes, and thank you." She had gleaming white teeth, beautiful brown skin. Her long, black, healthy-looking wrap made him want to run his hands through it. Her eyebrows arched, and she had deep, dark pupils like Tiffany from *In the House.*

"Thank you. I couldn't fuck with that line."

"Patience. Have to learn patience," she said.

"I want what I want now. So I work hard so I can have it like that. So what up? I don't need no drama in my life though, shorty." Dee reached down and rubbed her hand, then her ring finger.

"That's my husband's. He asked me to wear it. He's married. And drama don't come with this. Always a lady."

"What's your name, cutie?" Dee tried to stay in pimp mode, which was hard while rolling. The social, smooth, and sensual part of him began to come out. He was feeling the bitch and could tell she was feeling him.

"Lady—that's my name." She smiled.

"Yo' momma ain't name you Lady," Dee said with attitude.

"Wilma Lady Hill—don't tell me. What's your name?"

"Dee," he said as the fine-ass, light-skinned girl caught his eye. He seen her before. Where?

The girl looked at Dee and headed towards

him. Lady looked up at the girl coming. She stared as she walked up and hugged Dee as if she knew him.

"How you?"

"Fine and you?" He squinted his eyes to let her know he wasn't sure where he knew her.

"Monica—Angela's friend. I saw you earlier at the game. Didn't get a chance to meet you." Monica's team of girls looked on.

"Dee, a'ight."

"A'ight. Let me holla in a sec," he said putting her off, but she was fine. Then he remembered seeing her with dude sitting on the Benz. His mind started racing. Bedroom talk was a muthafucka.

He turned to Lady and assured her he would catch her before leaving.

Lady stepped off, but the look she gave Monica let her know she wasn't happy.

He quickly turned back to catch Monica's hand. "So what the deal? Your man let you out tonight?"

"Shit, he headed out of town."

"Niggas got to handle they business. You know how it is—money first."

"Yeah, when you the man, don't let niggas use you just to be down."

Dee could read Monica. She ran her mouth too much, trying to impress, like she knew something. So he pressed the issue as he moved to VIP. He ordered a bottle of Moët. He didn't like it, but the young hoes who weren't used to money thought it was something.

"So you just left your man home by himself and you bounced?"

"Naw. He home with his boys puttin' their little change together to go score."

Dee kept pouring. The champagne had her ass going. "What he buyin'? A ounce?" Dee laughed as if it was a joke.

"He talkin' about fifteen bricks," she said. "Fifteen bricks probably this big."

Dee knew them niggas had some paper. "I don't know why guys mess up money; they need to buy real estate. Buy a house; put that money there. Stop fuckin' it up, simple niggas."

"He got a big house."

"How big?"

"You seen them houses off Independence and Holland, that new complex. The ones in the back, the biggest. He got money."

"Guess so. So what's up with you? Goin' home from here? Or you hangin' out?"

"Tell me what's up?—I don't play for free."

"Whoa . . . I ain't got it like that."

"Then you playin'. Let me stroll a minute." Monica got up, and two girls from her crew followed.

Dee picked up the phone. He couldn't hear, so he walked out front. He called Black, but he wasn't answering. He dialed the condo.

Black knew nobody had that number, so it had to be important. "Yeah!"

"Shorty up here say her man home gettin' ready to score fifteen bricks.

"Who?"

"Yo' girl buddy, Monica. Her man, nigga with the CL drop."

"Ray?"

"I guess. He home with his mans and them with dough." Dee finished telling Black where the nigga lived and everything.

Black wasn't going out on a humbug, but he called Lo, told him to holla at Dundee and take a ride.

Lo called Dundee. When Dundee scooped Lo, he had Scotty with him. They drove out Holland Farms and rode around until they saw the drop-top Benz, a Q45, and Expedition.

They parked across the street, two houses down. They sat in the car with a 9mm, .45, and the shot-gun Scotty had.

Two guys pulled up in a Land Cruiser. One of the guys jumped out and ran inside.

"He waitin' on dude. As soon as he come out, we going in," Lo said.

"Let's do this, baby—my kind of shit," Scotty said.

Dundee sat not saying a word. This wasn't his type of shit. He sold drugs, not rob niggas, but he wanted to show niggas he was with anything.

They were so into going in the house, they thought nothing of the black, tinted Range Rover that rode by.

"How many niggas you think in there, Lo?" Scotty asked.

"Maybe three. Four at the most."

The other guy came out and got in the truck.

Within seconds of the truck pulling off, Scotty took the lead and knocked on the door. Lo was glad he came. This woulda got done without him, but Scotty and Lo had came up together, and when Lo got under Black, Scotty was robbing nig-gas like Black.

The door just opened—they thought the other guy had forgot something. Scotty put the shotgun in his chest and pushed him to the stairs.

Lo went to the left, Dundee to the right.

Dundee made two niggas get flat on the floor. Lo went through the living room to the kitchen and went upstairs the back way. He met Scotty at the room door.

They burst in the room over the garage. There stood Ray and some other cat.

"Bag it up, son," Lo said to Ray.

Ray began to bag slowly, praying the two nines didn't go off.

"He think it's a game, Lo," Scotty said, shotgun still in dude's chest.

Lo pointed the nine at the cat standing on the wall. *Pow*! He shot him in the chest. "You next," he said, busting Ray in the side of his head.

Ray gathered the money in the bag and walked downstairs with the cold steel sitting on the back of his neck.

As they hit the stairs, Lo yelled out to Scotty, who'd laid the guy down and slowly pulled the trigger to the shotgun. The sound scared Dundee, Lo, and the nigga coming in the door with the two .45's locked and loaded.

Lo kicked Ray in the back as he tumbled down the stairs, while the bullets from Lo's nines and Speed's .45's scattered.

Scotty ran down the back stairs, blasting a shot at the front. Speed jumped to the den, as him and Dundee exchanged gunshots. Dundee scattered to get away, catching a bullet in the foot.

Scotty bust another shot at Speed, takin' out the big screen. But two shots to Scotty's shoulder and neck left him in a puddle of blood.

Lo was shot in the thigh and stomach.

Dundee scrambled to the steps and grabbed the bag as the bullets came raining down.

Lo began shooting, and Speed pulled Ray away from Lo's shots.

Dundee saw this as the perfect time to make a run and dashed out the door, hopping and letting off shots at Speed and Ray. Ray fell from the stray that caught him in the spine.

The sirens got closer as Dundee sped away with Speed right behind him as they bypassed the police racing to the scene. Both cats were on paper and they had to leave. Neither could do anything for anybody locked up.

Speed musta turned off. Dundee raced down Independence and hit the interstate. He pulled in his driveway to the back of his house, went inside, and called Poppa.

Poppa never answered, so he counted the money. Three hundred thousand. *Damn! Jackpot!!!*

He tried Poppa again.

Dundee's phone rang. It was Poppa. He was at the Virginia Beach General when they brought Lo, Ray, Scotty, and the other two cats' bodies in.

"What happened?"

"Lo called me in to rob Ray. We bust in and scooped the dough. We gettin' ready to burst and Speed came through the door."

"Goddamn." Poppa closed his eyes and rubbed his forehead.

"He killed Scotty and Lo. I think I killed Ray."

"Lo got shot five times and he ain't dead," Poppa said. "Ray fucked up. Say bullet's in his spine. Scotty, Jake, and two more cats dead. For a couple hundred grand. Goddamn! Let me make a call and tell his peoples."

Poppa called Black and told him what had just happened.

Black said, "Call Dundee and tell him meet me at the apartment on Baker and to bring that money."

Dundee was sitting in the house, almost in tears when Poppa called. The fact that Scotty was gone had sunk in.

Dundee, Poppa, and Black stood on the balcony of the apartment. Black couldn't go to the hospital, and Dee wasn't answering his phone.

Black made the call he dreaded to make.

Tony T answered the phone.

Black let Lo's brother know what had happened so Moms and Auntie could go to Virginia Beach General. Then from every direction the red, white, and blue lights came flashing down Baker Road.

Dundee stood there and watched ten police cars surround his townhouse and kick in his door.

"Ray must of told. Thought I killed the son of a bitch."

"Well, you didn't. Now he puttin' the police on you. And they got Lo," Black said, digging for his phone that was ringing. "Yeah!"

"Fuck goin' on, stickman?" Speed said angrily.

"Fuck you mean, my nigga?" Black answered, his voice slightly raised.

"What y'all niggas fuck with my cousin for?" Speed lowered his voice. He had gotten real calm.

"I just heard about this shit—some beef carried over from the courts."

"Naw, baby. Yo' peoples robbed my cousin for three hundred thousand and left him in a wheelchair. Payback's a bitch, nigga."

"You better recognize who the fuck you talkin' to."

"Talkin' to you, son. Better soak it in, because when I see you we goin' to hell, baby. Straight to hell," Speed said and hung up.

"Where the other hundred thousand?" Black looked at Dundee.

"That's it—two hundred thousand. Word to my mother."

Black looked at Poppa and walked back inside. His phone rang. It was Tony calling from Virginia Beach General. Lo was going to be okay. Even though he got hit five times, there was no major damage.

Moms and Auntie had the staff in an uproar. They let them see Lo for a second. He did open his eyes. Tony told Black that all Lo said was three hundred thousand.

"There's police outside his door and they have him cuffed to the bed."

"Take care of Moms and Auntie," Black said hanging up. He looked at Dundee. "Lo said three hundred thousand. Speed said Ray said three hundred thousand. Speak now or live with your decisions."

"That's Lo's; I got my hundred." Dundee looked at Black as to say, "I'm not scared."

"Everybody think like that young nigga, but we are a clique. The only way we gonna have longevity and prosperity is to hold each other down. You ever lived like you livin' now?"

"Naw, man." Dundee looked at Poppa.

"Without me and Lo, this shit stops; with us, everything stays good in life—don't ever do that again. LE niggas . . . 'til we die."

"No doubt. Sorry," Dundee said. "You need to go get that foot checked," Poppa said.

"We all right, partner. Now we move forward." Black handed Poppa twenty-five thousand and kept the same for himself, putting the rest up.

Dundee hopped over to the couch. He told Black everything and how it went down. Now Black saw why he got up outta there. Now he knew Lo was going down for all that shit, because Ray was going to tell—it was his house and they had robbed him.

Chapter Eleven

Dee walked back in the club and ordered another double Henny straight and Corona. The bitches in the club was off the hook. The Ecstasy had him ready to freak, but the weed kept him from bouncing off the wall. He walked back to the second floor and found his VIP spot, sat down and ordered a bottle of Dom Perignon. He popped the champagne and poured a glass. He felt good.

He sat there watching as people came by, showing love that he hadn't seen in awhile, guys and girls. He realized then that the clubs in Atlanta was off the blinker, but it felt good to be home, to see niggas he'd been clubbin' with since Circle Bingo and Big Apple days.

Then two loud-ass niggas came up. Dee jumped up, hugging the niggas. It was Shawn and Smiley, two Norfolk hustlers who had a good piece of Norfolk and Portsmouth locked. Smiley was always a grimy money-getting nigga. Whatever was whatever. "Let's do it," was his attitude, as long as he got paid, and he always had a hustle.

Shawn was more laid-back, quiet type nigga. Got his money quietly, played fair, but if you ever got him wrong, sooner or later you got got. He usually ran with rich niggas, stars, and fucked a lot of ho's. "Fuck you been, nigga?"

"ATL, son." Dee shook his head.

"Heard the strip joints like no other," Shawn said.

"I'll come down there and have all those hoes callin' this dingy-ass Norfolk nigga Daddy. I heard them ho's got some paper," Smiley added.

"No doubt, kid. Houses, cars, jobs. It's poppin'," Dee said. "And all those gay niggas don't want no pussy."

"That's some bullshit." Shawn got a champagne glass and poured some Dom. "When you gonna open another sports bar?"

"As soon as you get some of your peoples to invest," Dee told him. "We'll do one for about one point two million. Have that shit bangin'."

"Well, we got four together. What you got?" Smiley asked. "I got four; all we need is four more. Shawn the man. All he got to do is go to Sweet Pea, Bruce Smith, Joe Smith, Allen *I*, Alonzo, Missy, Timberland."

"Goddamn, nigga, you fuck with everybody from Norfolk who done made it." Dee poured some more champagne in all three glasses.

"Dee, how many hoes you got in ATL, pimp?"

"I got two. I told myself I wa'n' goin' down there with all that, but you know, them hoes pulled me in," he said, giving niggas a pound.

Shawn pulled out a Dutch and split it, dumping the tobacco on the floor to roll the "labo" he had in his pocket. These niggas was gleaming—they had to have a hundred gees on in jewels between the two.

"I got four hoes. Real relationships with four hoes," Smiley said. "Keys to they houses, they cars—kids love me—and it's been goin' on for over seven years right here in Norfolk. So I know ATL callin' me."

Dee and Shawn laughed, but Smiley had a serious look.

"This the crazy part—I love all these hoes. People say it can't be done. But I'll kill a nigga over all four hoes."

"Tell him, Shawn."

Shawn shook his head in agreement and lit the Dutch.

"How many hoes you done fucked in Norfolk, Smiley?" Dee asked.

Shawn looked at Dee as if to tell him, "Don't get me started."

"About sixty in the last decade. What about you? I've seen you run hoes, Dee."

They both started laughing, remembering a time they'd bumped heads.

"Shit, I'll say about seventy or eighty," Dee said seriously.

"You ain't lyin', son. I know you. And I can say Shawn probably done fucked over a hundred hoes."

We laughed, but we both knew the hoes loved Shawn. They called him quiet and fine, and he was killing them all.

"So how you fuck four hoes like that. I fuck, but a nigga dick die out every now and then. Been fuckin' with that X—that shit make sex off the hook."

"I used to have that problem. Them old heads up at the Long Shoreman Hall turned me on to these." Smiley handed Dee two light-blue, diamond-shaped pills. "Viagra, nigga—for old heads who can't get hard and for young niggas who just want to fuck nonstop."

Dee looked at the pills and put them in his pocket.

"You got that X?" Shawn asked.

"All day long. AOL's, Mitsubishi, tweety birds. What?" Dee felt a deal coming on.

"Mad niggas doin' that shit, but it's hard to come by," Smiley said.

"Not no more. Twenty a pop all day," Dee said.

"I want a thousand," Shawn said.

"Twelve then. Tomorrow." Dee handed him one to try.

Shawn took it. "Tomorrow."

Just then Monica and her crew came by. Dee signaled for her to come over. They all came and began talking.

Dee was thinking he would like to fuck with this bitch. She was fine as hell. "So what?" he asked her in her ear as she leaned into him, "You want to get down?"

"One thousand and you got me all night."

Dee knew this bitch wa'n' getting a gee a night from niggas in Norfolk. "I don't want all night."

"Then five hundred from—" She looked at her watch. "It's one now . . . from now to six."

"Give me your number," Dee said as he put it in his phone. "I'll call you at three thirty. I want from four to five. You might make two hundred. I'm gonna hit you as soon as I get settled." Dee knew Ray wa'n' giving that bitch no real dough, still out here tricking.

He grabbed his dick, raising up from the table. He gave Smiley and Shawn a pound, telling Shawn, "Hit me up tomorrow."

"How y'all niggas know Dee? Y'all from uptown?" Monica asked.

Smiley smirked. "Who the fuck don't know Dee?"

"Niggas want to know his brother," Monica said.

"Whose his brother?" Shawn asked.

"Black."

"Black who? That Norview cat with the clothing store," Shawn said, "or Black from Grandy Park, or Black that run with Shampoo."

"Oh yeah," Smiley said, "Black from out Lake Edward. Back in the day they say he killed about ten New York niggas. Say he had mad bodies and never did a day."

"Okay, did he run with that nigga Lo with the dreads and the patch on his eye?" Shawn asked.

"Now remember when they found them two niggas at the mall dead, one in the back seat and one in the trunk."

"The nigga you talkin' about is Lo Max. Tall, black, skinny nigga with dreads. Wilder than a bitch."

Shawn looked at Smiley. "That's Dee peoples? That's why he always look like he flippin' keys with a asshole full of money."

"Because of his brother. I didn't know that shit."

"Come on," one of the girls said to Monica. "Broke-ass niggas not spendin' shit."

"Niggas ain't gonna spend shit with your nasty ass, bitch," Smiley said.

"Bitch, fuck you with your stinkin'-ass breath—that's why I moved."

"Bitch, you better recognize a pimp when you see one." Smiley jumped up and kicked her in the mouth with his Timbs.

Her head snapped back, just to catch a slap when it came back up. The slap took her off her feet.

Monica grabbed Smiley, and the other girl began hitting him.

Shawn grabbed the other girl by the hair, slinging her to the ground, and still holding her ponytail in his hand.

"Please, Smiley, don't beat her like that," Monica yelled as Smiley slapped the girl.

Monica was glad to see security grab Smiley. He turned on security and began head butting him until he let go. The other tried restraining him, and again Smiley grabbed him and began butting him across his nose until blood spread across his face.

Out of nowhere, Youngblood scooped Smiley up and slammed him to the ground. He tensed his body, but he went up again and the next slam took everything he had in him. He was cuffed and carried out.

Shawn was right behind them as they carried his man out. He was walking to the car mad as hell. "Security didn't have to do that."

He walked past a Quest van. Three niggas sat inside. "You need to tell Smiley to calm the fuck down."

"He'll be all right."

"That's why he got his ass whipped and your bitch ass let it happen."

"Fuck all you niggas."

They began laughing. They were drinking and smoking and joking so much, they never saw Shawn come back across the street from his car.

Pow! Pow! Pow!

Dee dropped to the ground in the parking lot. He was talking to Lady, trying to get her to roll with him, and saw when Smiley came out cuffed up.

Then he saw Shawn dash back across the street and his black, chromed-out Supra hit Independence Boulevard and disappeared.

Shawn left two kids dead in the Quest, and taught one kid a lesson—never fuck with niggas you don't know.

Dee knew it was time to go. He looked at Lady. All the sweet shit was over. "What you gonna do?"

She got in and they were out.

Dee took off towards his condo. Lady sat beside him, her right leg thrown across her left, leaving an exposed upper thigh that he couldn't help touching while she rambled on about how she'd been married four years, and her husband was a producer or some shit. He had a studio and was pushing mad artists. He offered her and their two kids the world but was never home, so she shopped and fucked up a great deal of his money.

They walked inside.

Dee decided he wanted to fuck hard if this bitch

gave him some pussy, so he walked in the kitchen and took one of the pills Smiley gave him to see how it worked. Then he poured himself a drink and sparked his Backwoods.

She sat there smoking her Newport cigarette.

He put on his Dave Hollister CD. By track 4 he had Lady laid back, kissing her neck and rubbing her breasts. He lifted her shirt and felt the lace bra that fastened in the front. The Ecstasy had him ready to freak.

As he kissed her neck, she began to moan and slide down in the sofa. He removed her blouse to see her beautiful breasts fill the gold bra. Lady stood in front of him in a gold bra, gold thong, and Chanel sandals, her diamonds gleaming.

Dee's dick was rock hard. He took her hand and guided her to his room.

She strolled to the bed with her ass jiggling.

Goddamn! His body felt so good, and his dick was throbbing. He removed his clothes down to his boxers. "Let's shower," he said, walking into his bathroom.

She undressed fully and stepped into the shower. He washed her down and she did the same.

When they came out and dried off, she pushed him back on the bed and began kissing his neck. It felt good, but she was sucking hard.

"Don't leave no marks on me," Dee said seriously.

"Don't worry, I won't," she said softly and kept kissing and nibbling until she reached his chest. She took his nipples into her mouth and sucked, then nibbled on the ends until she felt his heartbeat speed up. She reached down and stroked his dick. She knew he was ready the way his dick was jumping. She leaned down and placed her lips on his dick.

A sensation shot through his body.

She began sucking his dick like it was the best tasting piece of meat she ever had. The saliva ran down his balls into his ass cheeks. Lady kept sucking intensely as she massaged his balls. Then she turned him over with his ass in the air.

He flowed with it because she was making his body feel so incredible.

She got on her knees and pulled his dick back between his leg and sucked from behind.

"Whoa! Whoa!" was all he could mutter.

She kept going as she reached up and placed her finger on his asshole.

He jumped up and spun around. "Fuck is you doin'?"

"Oh! You never had a woman touch you there?"

"Hell naw. Don't fuck around."

"Look, Dee, relax. Aren't you secure with your sexuality? You know you ain't gay. I'm just playin', tryin' to make you feel good." Lady placed her head back on his head. Again she rubbed his balls until his knob was really wet. She laid him back, lifted his legs, and began to lick his balls, then his ass.

He jumped, but she kept going until sensations floated up and down his body. She eased her slim finger into his ass, and he shifted uncomfortably. Then she pressed her finger forward. Dee felt as if he was going to pee, but nothing happened.

Of all the bitches he'd fucked in his life, none ever made him feel this good. The feeling was rising from his feet through his body. He thought he was coming, then all of a sudden his entire body went numb. This feeling had his entire body shaking for about two minutes.

Lady sucked down every drop until he pushed her off his dick.

Dee laid there with a limp dick until he caught his breath. He felt like a bitch that had been turned out.

Lady lay on his chest and rubbed his stomach.

He wasn't pressed on no ass.

Then she grabbed his dick again. It rose instantly.

Damn! Dee took her in his arms and laid her back, climbed on top of her, and slid in.

Her pussy was burning up. It grabbed his dick and was pulling with every stroke. She brought her legs back real wide so he could get in tight and rub against her clit with every stroke. She began to buck wildly as he slammed his dick with authority until that feeling came again, and he let off a load to fill her up. Lady came at the same time too, and he collapsed in her arms.

"Damn, it's almost four o'clock. Let me go." Lady jumped and ran to the bathroom. She returned wearing her bra and thong. She walked back to the living room and slipped into her clothes. Then she kissed Dee and exited out the door.

Dee climbed in the shower and cleaned up. He went and laid in the bed and flipped on the TV. He grabbed his dick and squeezed it. He picked up the phone and hit Monica. "Hello."

"What's up, Dee?"

"You—let's do this; meet me at the Clarion."

"See you in about twenty minutes," she said and hung up.

Dee threw on his Pelle Pelle baby-blue velour sweatsuit and white DC's with the baby-blue stripe. He got to the Clarion and got a room. He took another Ecstasy pill.

She arrived and after smoking a Back, she tooted four times.

His X had just kicked in, and it was trick time. His dick throbbed at the thought of getting into this young girl.

She undressed, stood in front of him wearing a black bra and black thong on her red body.

He stood in the bed, holding his dick. "Crawl over here and suck this dick."

She crawled and sucked his dick, licked his balls. He even pulled his leg back and made her lick his ass.

He turned her over and slid in from the back. Every time he got excited and started pounding, she would slide up and keep him from getting deep.

He pulled her hair and her neck came back, as he slammed dick into her.

She wriggled until she broke his grip.

He picked her up and turned her on her back, grabbed his dick, and slid it into her, pushing his legs against hers so they would stay wide. Dee started bucking like a horse, cupping her under her shoulders and going crazy. He couldn't come, his dick hurt and throbbed, but it was rock hard. He kept going.

She yelled, "Stop! Stop!", and tried to push him off, but he heard nothing, felt nothing.

He fucked hard until his sweat dripped in her face. The tears ran as her pussy became dry and raw. The harder he fucked, the more she fought . . . until he finally bust. Out of breath, he collapsed thinking he might die.

She grabbed her clothes and headed out the door.

He lay there holding his rock-hard dick, feeling good. He was ready again.

Monica searched her caller ID on her cell, nervously looking for the number Angela had called from. *There it is.*

Her mind was in shambles. She rode past Ray's house and saw yellow tape around it. She ran home to catch Channel 5 news and heard about what happened at Ray's home. The announcer said, "The owner of the home was in Virginia Beach General in critical, but stable, condition."

Angela finally answered her phone. She was laying beside Black at the condo. She sat up. "What up, girl?"

"That muthafucka you fuck with, girl, is a beast. He's a fuckin' beast. He killed Fat Joe, and Ray laid up in the hospital now."

"Slow down," Angela said, her head racing.

"You said Fat Joe—Oh my God—and what?" Angela wasn't about to say Ray's name while Black was lying next to her.

"Yeah, Ray's fucked up too. Scotty died. It was on Channel 5. Yo' nigga did this because of that shit."

"Kill it, girl—you reachin'."

"Ask him. That was Fat Joe; we grew up together, Angela," Monica cried. "All of us, from Bayside Elementary to Bayside Middle to Bayside High." She cried even harder.

Angela felt her pain. She was hurt, but she never fucked Fat Joe like Monica did. *And what the fuck was he doing around Ray house anyway?*

"Ask him. You know I'm right. I'm going to the hospital to check on Ray; you owe him that much."

I ain't owe Ray shit. "Bye," Angela said.

"Are you goin'?" Monica asked.

"Yeah, I'll see ya." Angela hung up the phone and looked at Black. "Something happened."

"Yeah, I saw it on Channel 5."

"Saw what?" Angela tried to see what he knew.

"Tone down, girl." Black held his left hand out, showing a down motion.

"My best friend from childhood is dead. My girl is fucked up. I got to go check on some things."

He got out the bed and slipped on his boxers and wife-beater. He picked up his Back and pulled on it. "I don't care where you go or what you do, but don't interfere in that street shit and don't go visiting at the hospital." Black knew the police was watching who was coming and going.

Angela stopped at the bathroom door. "Why not, Strong? Tell me why?"

"Just don't—now leave it alone." He was tired of the conversation.

"Fuck that. You—"

Next thing you know, her naked body was pinned against the wall between the dresser and the bathroom door. She was on her tiptoes, the dresser pushing into her side, and his hand around her neck and pushing against her windpipe.

She blacked out for about five seconds. When her vision became clear, her eyes were wide, her mouth open, and her skin was darkening.

"Don't ever challenge me. You haven't been around long enough." Black threw her body across the bed, making her body slam against the oak headboard.

She jumped up and stood on the bed. "I'm tired of muthafuckas puttin' they hands on me." She charged across the king-size bed.

He grabbed her neck and tossed her as he moved to the side, but her momentum made her fall through the closet door. "Bitch, you don't know who you fuckin' with," he said, picking up his Backwoods. "Now clean this shit up." He walked downstairs and stood in his family room and looked through the clear glass at the waves rushing the shore.

"Black, I can't be goin' through this. I love you, but I can't. I'm gonna leave the keys to the truck and catch a cab." She stood at the banister overlooking the family room.

"I said you weren't goin' because the police is probably watchin' everybody goin' in and out. You get hot, Black gets hot. Strong ain't wanted, but Black been locked up twice and is wanted in three states. Black got two felony charges. If they catch Black right now he'll be gone a long time. Strong loves you. But Black will put two in your muthafuckin' head and be gone in sixty sec," he said, still looking over the water, and pulling on his Back, never turning around. "Before he get locked up behind your ass."

She walked back in the room and began cleaning up. She couldn't believe what she had just gone through. But she did know two things—she wasn't going to the hospital; and she wa'n' leaving her muthafuckin' truck.

Chapter Twelve

Kev was supposed to be in Memphis, but he spent more time in VA with Black, waiting for his move farther South and had become accustomed to VA. Him and Dee were on their way by the hospital to check on Poppa's situation. They were getting off the elevator and ran into Monica.

"What's up, Monica?"

"I can't fuck with you—you are dangerous."

"What the hell you talkin' about?"

"You know what you did," she said. "I know."

Kev leaned closer to her. "Be concerned if you want, but don't let your mouth make your whole body end up in a canister floatin' in the Dismal Swamp. Be careful, Monica."

"I know that nigga ain't givin' you shit, or you wouldn't be trickin'. Let me tell ya how you can put fifty grand in your pocket," Dee added.

Her eyes popped open. It seemed as if the anger was gone. She shut her mouth and stepped on the elevator, shook.

Dee decided to carry his ass home. He had

thought about staying home, letting her come over, but she just fucked Ray. She wa'n' gettin' him, triflin' bitch.

He was tired, so he punched the Ferrari. As he flew past Witchduck Road, two state troopers sat on the right. He looked at his speedometer—100. He knew he was going to jail.

They shot out after him.

He got off on Newtown, but by the time he reached the Boulevard, they had him. He got a reckless driving, eluding the police, no seat belt, and they towed the Ferrari.

They carried him to Princess Anne.

It was 6:00 then; he didn't get a call 'til 10.

Dee finally got in touch with Black. He sent Tony to bail him out. His bail was set at ten thousand. Tony gave the bondsman one thousand and Dee walked. He had to pay one fifty for towing.

Black took the car and keys, but he gave Dee forty-five thousand for schooling them on Ray. At least that made him smile.

Dee rode over to Bayside Hospital. Moms and Auntie was there. It was Sunday and the restaurant was closed. Auntie assured us that he was out of danger and he was going to be okay.

Kev was ready, so he picked him up with Dream. She was looking rough, but she was there for Kev, with the badges on the side of his face. They went to his crib to clean up and shower.

He left Dream there, while him and Dee ran to check on Lo. After he heard what happened, he was even more outraged. He had never witnessed so much drama in a day.

They pulled in front of the hospital. Poppa was standing in the front looking like a zombie. They'd forgot his girl was still here.

"You a'ight, Poppa?" Kev asked.

"Girl slipped in a coma. What I do to deserve this?" Poppa said.

Big, strong-ass nigga wiped his eyes. Kev couldn't understand, but Dee could. Dee had lost a girl before, and he knew Poppa was scared. He felt for him, but words meant nothing at this time. His life mate was in trouble, and it was nothing nobody could do or say at this time.

Dee and Kev walked upstairs to check on Lo. The police was outside the door and they wouldn't let them visit. Dee didn't have ID and Kev was too stressed to argue.

They walked back downstairs. Poppa was gone, so they got in the whip and headed back to Black's condo.

They must of rode for fifteen minutes in the Dodge Intrepid listening to the sounds of some underground shit by Fifty.

"Stop lookin' so sad, son. You still pretty," Dee said.

"I know. I just feel fucked up inside," Kev said.

"Why? The nigga that did that paid for it—with his life. That's done."

"You right. Just feel funny."

"Need to chill, kid. Everybody ain't built for this shit—day-in-day-out hustlin' . . . not knowin' what the next day gonna bring. If you find a nigga that's been in this shit for ten years or better, he's cold and he built for shit most niggas can't stand. This shit ain't easy. You got to be smart, stay ahead of the game, get money, and— most of all—stay alive.

Niggas who fuck with this shit crazy and you better know it."

"Dee, you smart as hell. You ever killed any-body?"

"I've caught three in my lifetime," Dee said slowly. "Two over bitches and one over my brother. The one over Black, I dropped him point-blank range, to the back of the dome in the club. I will never forget how his body fell. I see it over and over, but it doesn't bother me, because I did that to protect Black. I'll do that anytime. My brother's all I got.

"The two over them ho's keep me fucked up. Young niggas like you let that pussy get them open and they lost their mind. Now one was ready to take my life. The other I think was trying to be hard and show out. Never pull a burner to play—this lifestyle is not a game; it's a way of life.

"So why keep playin' in it? You don't even sell drugs."

"The richest niggas sell drugs. There's many other hustles that get you close to that money. Do what you know. And I stay close in the game be-cause of the money, bitches, cars, the respect that comes with the car you drive, the money you got, and the bitch on your arm. I been here too long. I love the 'not knowing what tomorrow brings.'"

They pulled up to Black's condo, where they saw the Black Yukon Denali XL, parked with hand-icap plates, from New Jersey.

Kev knew who it was. He knew what he was fac-ing. They walked inside. Kev walked over and hugged his cousin.

"Look what happens when you out of my care," Polite said.

"We goin' home, son. I'm gonna go back and forth for a second, but you can handle Memphis. Me and Strong gonna work somethin' out. Bring 'em in to Tennessee from Atlanta. We'll be a'ight." Kev felt good. He knew he'd still be with Black. *Only a phone call away.* He loved Polite, but he learned from Black.

"You not leavin' for a couple weeks, let's get Lo back and rollin'. Check this out."

They all walked to the table.

"We'll show Lo and Poppa before you leave. You gonna bring your peoples, Pop and them, in under Poppa. Grip just got picked up on that kid's murder. Somebody said he thought the kid was snitchin', so he was going to do him. When they stopped him, he had a half brick of 'hard' (crack). I don't know if he talkin' or what. And Speed fuckin' up. I don't know what he doin'. So this is the change. We changing the cribs out LE that they been to. We got three cars—each gonna have a stash. We meet at the malls, Wal-Mart's, big parking lots. Park on opposite sides, go in the store, and swap keys. No more hand to hand—key to key, car to car."

Dee looked on. *Real smooth.*

Kev thought it was good also.

Polite just realized how he was going to run Memphis. "I'm goin' to Memphis tomorrow. I'll see you in two weeks. Now let's find a restaurant."

They all left out, jumping in the Denali XL.

Black called Angela, and her and Dream met them at Piccadilly. Dee called Stacy. She was there in a flash.

* * *

They finished eating and walked outside. Dee walked the girls to the truck. They were getting ready to head back to the ATL. They both had work Monday morning.

"Y'all should be getting' back about one," Black said. He walked over to Angela.

She hugged him. "When will you be home?" She held him tight.

"About three weeks—in time to close the house. Go ahead and put down the deposit and sign the papers for the one we picked."

"Be careful, Black." She smiled. "I can't lose you."

"You won't. Don't you worry, you won't."

Kev stood on the other side of the truck in deep thought with Dream.

"I don't believe in that corny shit—love at first sight and all. But I've never enjoyed myself with anybody Kev like I did this weekend—minus the craziness. I never thought VA was like this."

"Know what, they say VA is for lovers. I guess you found that out."

"They need to say VA is for hustlers. Because y'all niggas is gettin' it." She pulled him closer and kissed him, throwing her tongue around in his mouth.

He kissed her back, not giving a fuck about all the church folks coming and going.

"Look, Dream, I'm gonna be straight. I want you to go to Atlanta and straighten out all your personal shit . . . because I'm comin' in a couple weeks."

"All right, Kev. There's nothin' to clear up. My

plate is clean—school, work—and I want you to
know my door is open to you."

"I'll be goin' to Tennessee in a couple months.
Once I plant my roots, I want you there. Think
about it; we'll talk later." He kissed her again, and
they hugged.

Black and Dee watched as their girls rolled away
in the G5 truck, looking pretty, headed for the
ATL.

It was Sunday night—reggae night at Club Ritz
on Military Highway. Bitches were off the hook.

Polite, Kev, Black, Dee, and Poppa were sitting
at a table drinking and talking business.

Poppa was looking sad because his girl hadn't
gotten any better.

Black was staring into space. He wanted to go
home and climb next to Angela. The two days she
was home had spoiled him.

Kev was sipping on his Hennessy and deep in
thought.

"What y'all think of this club?" Poppa asked.

"It's all right. Nice crowd," Dee said.

"I know the niggas. They ask me to come in and
get down for a third," Poppa responded.

"How much?" Black asked.

"A hundred gees."

"Shit ain't bringin' in that much," Kev said.

"It's okay. I see makin' it back. I need an invest-
ment," Poppa said.

"Talk to this attorney and this accountant before you do anything. Let them say it's a good deal,
and draw up paperwork to make sure you get

yours back and everything is legit." Dee handed
Poppa two cards.

Polite asked, "So VA still wild as hell?"

"Yeah, this shit off the hook," Mike-Mike said.
"Poppa gettin' ready to buy the club—free liquor
and free beer all night."

Everybody started laughing because they knew
he was serious.

Black had his eyes glued to the door, with all the
beef going on. He wasn't comfortable at all.

"Heard you got locked up, Dee," Mike-Mike
said. "Fastest car in the world and you stop.
Muthafuckas wouldn't have got me." He acted out
a getaway.

Stacy walked up with three of her friends. Dee
had called her. He wanted the company of this
young, beautiful, innocent-ass girl. She spoke, and
Dee walked them to the bar, with Polite rolling beside one. We later found out that he could still
fuck; his dick wa'n' paralyzed.

"How Lo doin'?" Poppa asked.

"He gonna be okay after we see what the police
gonna hit him with," Black said.

"That Ray nigga gotta go—he's the one who
gonna fuck around and put Lo away," Kev said,
feeling like if he killed someone he'd feel better
about his life, his face, and his fucked up heart.

"Where Dundee?" Black asked. "Did you take
care of that?"

Black had told Poppa to give Dundee his apartment he had for tricking. Poppa didn't really use it
since his girl had been down; he was always with
her since her complication earlier in her preg-
nancy.

Dundee needed a low spot. The police was on a manhunt for him. A two-time felon, he had three murders and wasn't about to give up his whole life to get locked up.

"Yeah, he straight. He over there with Pee-Wee. You know without Scotty they fucked up," Poppa said.

"Feel you," Kev said.

Then they heard a phone ring.

It was like a chain reaction, as everyone grabbed their phone.

Dee answered.

"Hey, baby. What you doin'?"

"Sittin' in the club, sippin' on some syrup, listenin' to the sounds."

"You need to call me back," Tricia said; "I got some news for you."

"Holla. What's up?"

"I haven't seen a period in two months."

"So we need to handle this shit soon." Dee loved her but didn't want any more kids right now.

"Handle what?"

Dee walked to the room with pool tables and couches so he could hear better. He wasn't expecting this conversation tonight.

"You ain't havin' another baby right now. Barely take care of the one you got. This ain't the time. You better set up an apartment. Shit, I care for you, but I don't love you like that."

Actually he did love her, but he had to convince her not to have this baby. He didn't want that now, and plus, how the fuck could he tell Chantel this? Shit, fuck all those other hoes—Chantel was going to go off. There was no way this could happen.

"You can fuck around and have it. I'll take care of it if it's mine, but I'm not gonna be there. You on some bullshit."

"Fuck you mean 'if it's yours'?" she said loudly. "You know goddamn well I haven't fucked anybody else. You are a sorry-ass nigga. I would of never thought you'd act like this."

Dee felt bad. He knew she hadn't fucked anybody.

"I ain't gettin' no fuckin' abortion. I ain't killin' my baby." Tricia screamed. "My momma raised four of us by herself; I can do two."

"Fuck all that shit you talkin'. I'm out." Dee hung up.

She called back several times, but he never answered.

His mind stayed on Tricia. She was beautiful, and a wonderful homemaker. He knew she would be a great mother to his child. It suddenly hit him that he actually wanted a child. His only daughter was almost ten and a brand new baby would be something great. Here he was telling Tricia to get an abortion, not because of timing, but because he didn't want to hurt Chantel, who'd been trying unsuccessfully to have his baby for the last year. Then here comes this young girl who shows love like no other woman, takes care of him like no other, and he wants to put her through hell because of his love for another woman.

Damn! His mind was racing. He looked at his phone and a feeling ran through his body. He was scared to answer. He felt like shit as he watched the phone ring until it read "1 CALL MISSED." He noticed his team rushing out the door and ran outside.

Poppa was on the ground beside his Suburban, balled up, his hands over his face, and crying like a baby.

Black and Kev tried to help him to his feet, but he had no strength. He jumped up and put his fist through his driver side glass, before he leaned against the truck and continued to cry.

"What's goin' on?" Dee asked running up.

"His girl just died. Her aunt just called," Black told him.

Stacy and her crew walked outside to see what was going on. "What's wrong, Dee?" she asked. "Is everything okay?"

"No. My people's girl just died—his baby moms."

"This been a hell of a weekend. Y'all won't never forget *this* Fourth."

"Never," Dee said. "Somebody need to drive him down to Virginia Beach General."

Kev took his keys and helped him in the passenger side, and he and Mike-Mike carried him to the hospital. He had stopped crying and fell into a deep stare. His eyes were swollen.

For the thirty-minute ride all Poppa did was stare straight through the windshield, never blinking an eye.

They reached the hospital and ran upstairs. As he headed to the room Princess was in, he met her mother.

"Where were you?"she scolded. "My daughter died lovin' your no-good ass—you ain't shit."

Poppa walked past her and fell into the arms of Princess' aunt. They hugged as more tears fell.

Her mother was going on and on, crying and fussing about Poppa not being any good.

Finally Kev stepped up. "How you think Poppa

feel? You lost a daughter, but he lost the mother to his two kids, and his wifey. He left here to raise two little kids. You need to chill out and be considerate."

"Fuck that! He ain't raisin' shit. I'm takin' those kids—he won't even fuckin' see them."

Poppa lifted his head.

"You's a ignorant bitch," Mike-Mike said.

"No you—" was all that came out of her mouth before she felt the back of Mike-Mike's hand.

"Shut up. Poppa doin' everything in the world to show you respect. I don't know you and don't give two fucks about you. Now carry that shit outta here."

She ran down the hall, screaming her peoples or somebody was going to kill everybody and Poppa.

Dee was headed to his condo with Stacy. Her crew had gone to the hotel with Polite and Black.

Stacy entered the condo and was very much impressed. "So who house is that in Church Point by my grandparents?"

"Mine. All mine."

She made herself comfortable. "I heard that."

They sat down. He poured some Hennessy and lit his already rolled Backwoods. He was in deep thought as he took long pulls. He stared at Stacy. He could only push her away for so long.

Stacy wanted Dee and she wanted all of him. She didn't want to play as she told him, but he took it to heart and wasn't pursuing her.

She had on her tight black jean shorts, white top that tied in the front and exposed her belly, and black and white Nikes.

He passed her the Back.

She took her pulls, sat it in the ashtray, and

leaned over to kiss him. She was scared, and it showed; she had never been so forward.

But Dee met her, took her in his arms, and began kissing her from her lips to her neck. He undid her shirt and unsnapped the bra. Her beautiful breast fell out and he began sucking them, easing her out of the tight Liz Claiborne shorts.

He wasn't pressed for this, but he wanted it since it was here to get.

He had on his velour sweatsuit with an elastic waist, so his dick was out in seconds. After pulling her panties to the side, he pushed his dick to her entrance, looking in her eyes as he pushed.

She opened her legs and slid back on the couch. "It's been a while."

He looked into her dazzling brown eyes and cute face that looked so young and innocent. The deeper he stared, the more he realized that she wasn't a freak. She was a young woman in search of love: a pleasant young man doing something with himself, who would be there for her mentally, spiritually, and sexually. She wanted the same thing Chantel, Vianna, and Tricia wanted.

He had too much on his plate. So why pull her into all that? Just show her how the nigga she do decide to fuck with should treat her.

He stood up and pulled her into the bedroom and removed her shoes and panties. He ran some hot bath water in the Jacuzzi tub. He bathed her as the jets massaged her body. He dried her down and applied lotion to her, massaging her body from neck to toe. She was lying on her stomach, so he pulled her to her knees and pushed her chest and face to the bed. So her ass would be high up, exposing every bit of the fresh, inviting pussy.

Her clit was larger than most, so as he flicked his tongue across it she jumped. Then finally the slow licks from her clit to her ass relaxed her until she fell into a world of pleasure. No nigga had ever licked her like this.

Dee's tongue slid in and out of her wet pussy. He positioned his mouth so he could use his top lip to push up the skin that covered the clit and he sucked lightly so the clit came out as he ran his tongue in a slow circular motion. He felt her breathing getting harder and speeded up the motion until she lost control. Her legs went further back and got wider and she grabbed the top of his head and the moaning began. He felt her about to come, could taste her pleasant juices flowing, so he sucked again on the skin covering the clit as his tongue roamed.

He placed a finger inside of her as he continued to eat her. Her pussy kept squeezing his finger. She was ready. He stood and removed his Polo boxers and slowly slid into her tight vagina—even with the wetness.

She caressed him as if she had never felt anything so good.

He took several strokes, cupped her head into his arms, as he stared into her face. He slowed down, gaining control.

She opened her eyes; he stared deep into hers and the feeling began to run. From his feet, up his leg, through his penis, and kept going until his eyes shut and his body went numb.

He collapsed, rolled over, and she slid up under him. He hugged her and realized she felt real good.

* * *

The next couple months were hectic. Poppa's girl dying left him fucked up and fucking up. He wasn't on time for shit. He was like a zombie. His girl mom's was putting him through hell. She had him in and out of court trying to keep his kids. She was going off at the funeral—she even tried to spit on him.

Lo was moving again. He was moving slow, but he kept his nines close by. He was out on a five-hundred-thousand-dollar bond. Black took fifty thousand from him and Dundee's robbery, gave it to Brandy, who was there to bail him out. Brandy had been with Lo before his last bid on his last good run. He treated her good—and a lot of other hoes—but whenever he seemed to get into some shit, she was there to pull his ass out.

Lo was charged with breaking and entry, two counts of murder. His biggest problem was the firearm he had. He was a felon—automatic five years.

Then he had Ray to worry about. He was going to testify and that would put him away for sure, especially if he rolled up in a wheelchair. He had a court date for late November, but the attorney assured us he wouldn't see the courtroom until sometime in 2000.

Kev had gone to Memphis. Him and Polite were running things there. They met Black every other week in ATL. That made up for the money Mont and Grip was bringing. Shawn and Smiley called. Black had them scoring from Lo. JaVonne had got

down. He was from around the way and didn't respect Poppa as a hustler, but he would buy from
Lo. No money had ever stopped.

Black and Dee stood in the middle of Black's living room with the high ceilings, wide foyer, with
the three-hundred-thousand-dollar chandelier. He
had an elevator in his house that went up to the
second floor. Six bedrooms, five full baths, three-
car garage, family room, formal dining room,
game room, pool, workout room, office, closed-in
deck with Jacuzzi. $1.7 million dollars well spent.

At first Black said he was gonna get some hoes
and decorate, but he didn't want them knowing
where he lived. The idea was quickly dismissed
when Dee introduced him to Yvonne Jasline
Taylor. She was 33, graduate of Temple University
in Philadelphia, PA and was becoming known as
one of the top interior designers in the state.

Dee had met her at Homeorama. She had won
the contract to design all the homes up at
Homeorama. He began talking. She was used to
dealing with more white folks, so to work for some
young black brothers was going to be a challenge.
They didn't know the name of all the fancy shit,
but Dee and Black knew what they liked.

When she first met Dee at his $750,000 home in
Church Point, she was all business. Pants suit,
heels, hair in a bun with Liz Claiborne eyewear.
She carried big books to show her work and give
ideas. Dee sat for six hours picking out shit for
every room. She charged one hundred and fifteen

dollars an hour for consultation, and started him a running tab, meaning pay for everything later.

She finished the living room and dining area and we were at eight thousand for window treatments, matching dining chairs, and vases and shit. By the time the house was finished another hundred thousand was spent. And the house was laid like a model. She took pictures for her book to show future clients.

When she met Black it was like straight chemistry. They began talking and exploring his home at 10 A.M. They finished after 10 that evening. They talked business. A lot of business.

Lunchtime, since it was a beautiful day, he asked Yvonne to move her ML 500 Benz truck, so he could pull out the Ferrari. They rode up the to the coast to Virginia Beach Resort, went inside to the Tradewinds, four-star restaurant that overlooked the Chesapeake Bay.

She was impressed. He was like no other client she'd dealt with. Cats in the music industry always talked about themselves, bragging about what they're getting ready to do. Those ball players think everybody want them, but Black, he listened.

If he agreed he let her know, if he didn't feel it, he let her know before she wasted all her breath. He was direct, but he also wanted her feel.

The beauty of the home was picture-perfect, her best work. She didn't only take pictures, but it sparked an idea to walk through the home and put it on video. Black's home was plastered in *Home* magazine, *Robb Report, Millionaire.* With all her education, success, and her jump in lifestyle, that nigga Black had her open.

"So where's Yvonne?" Dee asked, sparking a Back.

"She should be through in a little bit. Let's go in the game room with the trees."

"Can't smoke in your own shit, nigga."

"You know the deal—shorty treat it like it's hers. She also made that ninety-one hundred mortgage payment last month."

"Yeah, let's go in the game room," Dee said smiling. "So what's goin' on? When you goin' back to the ATL?"

"Shit, I don't know. Poppa still fucked up. He can't run like he want to because social service makin' sure he on point with those kids."

"I would of probably had somebody kill that bitch," Dee said. "Send Lo and Dundee."

"Shit, they a fuck it up—don't even know how to rob a nigga."

They laughed.

"How things workin' out with Shawn and your boy?"

"They comin', DaVonne comin', and those young New York niggas peoples got tore off. Them niggas scorin' from Dundee now. Them little niggas workers. When you goin' to ATL?"

"Couple days I'm goin' to Cali with Vianna. So I'm going to Charlotte, then to the ATL, burstin' Friday morning. Cali . . . going back to Cali." Dee gave Black a pound.

Dee shook his head. "Man, shorty pregnant,"

"Who? Tricia?"

"How you know?"

"She called me, cryin', talkin' twenty miles per hour for about twenty minutes."

"Damn! She loves you, son. Bitches know a real man. She see it all in you."

"Yeah, but one thing—Chantel. Man, fuck! I live and breathe that girl. If everything a'ight there, I'm okay; if shit fuck up there, I can't even get a peace of mind."

"Yeah, but you only got one child. You gettin' too old to be killin' babies."

"She said she ain't, anyway. She said her moms did four by herself, she can damn sure do two."

They both smirked at her boldness.

"Guess you ain't got no choice."

"I guess not. Where the girls?"

Black had picked his daughter and Dee's daughter up. They had grown so fast. "Nine years old, looking like little ladies," Black said when he picked them up Friday night.

They were in the back whispering, like they were having their own private conversation going. They decided they were going to live with Black. Dee's daughter said he had more than enough room. Black's daughter said everybody could live there—her, her sister in Florida, her cousin, and even her mom.

They had spent Saturday up at the restaurant with grandma, and since the restaurant had opened, they were getting their hair done at NY Hair Designs, two doors down. So all day they ran from the restaurant, to the beauty salon, looking beautiful as ever with their long hair hanging down their backs, dressed cute as hell in jean sets, new white Reebok Classics.

They ran back to the beauty salon, bursting inside.

"Y'all not goin' to be runnin' in and out. Come here!" Leah, the shop owner, said. She sat them down, talking to them.

Dee always loved when she took the time and showed them special attention. She was someone for them to look up to and model themselves after. She was young, beautiful, owned two businesses, and had a Lexus that let every nigga know she DO4SELF.

They listened then jumped up.

Thirty minutes later they were back at the shop, until grandma threatened to find a switch.

The little ladies hauled ass in the room with their dads. No warning of any sort. Just burst in the room, interrupting the conversation.

"Heah, Daddy."

"Heah, Uncle Dee."

"What up, little ladies?" Dee hugged them.

"What y'all doin'?"

"Playing my PlayStation."

"I heard y'all runnin' up and down the stairs. Better be careful. I don't got time to sit at no hospital. If you fall and bust your head, I'm going to give you a towel and leave you here."

"Daddy, you crazy."

"We ain't gonna get hurt; we know what we doin'."

"Y'all get outta here—we smokin'," Black said.

They ran out excited and happy, just like kids should be.

"They somethin'," Black said.

"Yeah, I know. Just pray their life goes well."

"We ain't worried; they straight—we gonna make sure of that."

"Yeah, but a parent never know what they child have in store or how they will turn out."

"You right, but we'll leave that in the hands of God. Just pray for them."

"Like Momma do?"

"Just like Momma. Shit, I know it's her prayers that keeps me here. Damn sure ain't mine. No more time than I give the Lord."

"Need to start goin' to church with Tony, Momma, and Auntie."

"Yeah, Tony the godson. He ain't fuckin' with this shit here," Black said. "He's gonna make something of himself. For sure."

"Hell yeah, goin' to Regency University. Military payin' for it. Studyin' theology. He got God on his side. How can he lose?"

"Strong, Strong," they heard the voice hollering.

"We in here," Black yelled. He opened the door.

Yvonne walked into the smoke-filled room. "Y'all know the girls here."

"They know what we do. Wait 'til y'all have me a nephew. He gonna know too." Dee knew that kind of talk would aggravate her.

"I'll be goddamn!"

They laughed, but not at her.

"You wanna go to Cali for three days? Leavin' Friday."

"Hell yeah. I ain't never been to California," she said.

"You scared of those Cali hoes—they'll eat your ass up." Dee said joking.

"Can't no bitch fuck with it. Don't let the Chanel and long hair fool you. Better recognize how this Philly bitch get down," she said turning up her nose.

"Dee and Vianna goin' to Cali," Strong said. "Her job."

"What about Chantel?" she asked.

"We ain't ask you all that. You goin'?"

"Yes, I am. I ain't lettin' Strong go out there with you. You are corrupt. Don't fuck up my man." She hugged Black.

"I got to get ready to go before traffic get bad." She was taking the girls shopping. She enjoyed them. She didn't have any kids of her own yet, and spoiling them was something she loved; and telling them things about being little ladies. She even let them hang when she went to the spa. The ladies gave them little robes, and put clear polish on their feet and nails. They never wanted to go home when it was time.

"Yo, I talked to Lo and them earlier. Niggas gonna pull the bikes out—nice-ass day. What's up? Pull out the triple X," Dee said, referring to Black's Honda 1000.

"Got shit to do. Some of us gotta work. This good life don't come easy." Black waved his hand around, bringing attention to his extravagant home.

"I say that's for sure. But straight up, son, you got enough dough to chill. You can go wherever, put down new roots, and live comfortable forever. I got some new shit for us anyway. Gonna make us millions." Dee finally got the nerve to tell his little brother it was time to change their way of living.

"Where that shit come from? We livin' better than we ever have. Things rollin' good—fuck you talkin'."

"You got a heavy-duty high security safe with half-inch solid steel reinforced doors holdin' over three million upstairs. You got a safe at my house holding one and a half million. You got a safe in your condo with a couple hundred thousand.

Then Triple Strong is worth—what—another four or five. You done came off. Look, this is the plan—go to Atlanta and start Triple Strong Building Corp. Buy land, build houses, and sell. Spend six hundred thousand and sell for one point two million—real flip."

"Shit sounds good. Do your thing. I'll send Angela to real estate school. She ain't doin' shit anyway, sniffin' her ass off, spendin' up my goddamn money. She brings home like nine hundred every two weeks, but she spends two thousand a week. Know what, Dee, this shit is me. It's not just the money, it's the game—I love it. I love the players, I love the streets, I enjoy the fear I put in niggas, not knowin' what the fuck I'm gonna do. I love goin' to the parties with all the rap artists and entertainers, and I shine."

"You ain't got shit to prove. Most of them niggas rappin' about the life you live or life I live ballin' with these bitches drivin' hundred-thousand-dollar cars." Dee smiled.

"You know the greatest nigga was B.I.G., and the realest nigga is Fifty."

"Where Pac fit in?"

"I ain't no Pac fan, so I put couple niggas before him, startin' with Jiggah. Black, I love this shit too—having the homes, cars, bikes, jet-ski and enough money to do whatever I want with these hoes. But I want to know that we gonna grow old and be hangin'. Come pick each other up, play golf. I don't know. Just get old."

Black knew what he meant but he was a hustler. He loved the thrill of game, never to be separated from Dee, or the streets.

"Don't worry, we gonna be a'ight," Black assured him.

"A'ight. Love ya, man." Dee hugged his brother and made his exit.

He was on his way to his condo when Monica called. She was still upset about things, but she wanted to know more about the fifty thousand.

They pulled out the bikes and met Monica at the restaurant. She was back in with Ray and he had moved. She was helping him adjust to being in a wheelchair. One of the bullets had ruptured his spinal cord and disabled him from the waist down.

She told Dee where Ray lived and who was there with him. He might even get lucky and catch Speed there. Dee called Black.

Ray had to go because his testimony was going to put Lo away for a long time.

By the time Dee finished his conversation, many other bikes had joined him. Some of the guys were even riding girls. Dee looked at Monica, looking sexy in her tight jeans and black boots. She could definitely ride.

"So you ride?" he asked.

"Yeah, I'm ridin' with you." she answered while going to lock her car. She put on Dee's extra helmet.

They never noticed the black Range Rover parked in front of Food Lion.

Black called Lo. He knew this had to be done right. Lo decided he wanted to call Dundee, who let Black know that he was ready, not only to be brought in on this, but also to be offered better prices and a promotion to it.

Dundee was on the run and still moving six

kilos a week, three from his cousins in Carolina and three he worked. He stayed in the street two to three days straight; not washing, rocking the same clothes, grinding.

Black met them at Lo's spot, and they rode over to Ray's new ranch-style duplex with ramps and shit, off Witchduck Road, called Witchduck Lakes. He'd bought a beige Mercury Mountaineer with special attachments to drive.

They watched as they rode past the house. It was two others in the home. Lo was turning around at the end of the street when he saw the black Range Rover coming down towards Ray's house.

"Bingo, niggas," Black said. "This me. I'm gonna catch him goin'." He jumped out the truck and ran through the houses.

When Speed put his keys in Ray's door and saw Black coming up, he panicked—he had left his gun in the truck. He was only gonna be there a second. His eyes widened as he took off, his body hitting the corner of the house as he ran like a cheetah.

Black was hot on his tail. He'd caught him slipping and he had to go.

As Speed dodged between the cars and buildings, Black had the nine out, one in the chamber. Speed ran back by the dumpster, not knowing his surroundings.

Black was the only nigga name he had heard ring in the streets like his. When you heard Speed or Black, real niggas put up their guards, and bitch niggas broke out.

Two bullets ripped through his black leather Nautica, and he fell on the cold concrete, leaning against the dumpster. *How could I slip like this?* The cold steel that now rested on his temple let him know it didn't make a difference.

Black pulled the trigger and watched his body go totally limp, then he ran back to the house.

Dundee and Lo were already inside. They had a nigga and a girl flat on the floor in the kitchen. Ray was sitting in his chair with Lo's .357 to his head.

Black shut the door. "We got like two minutes. Where the money, nigga?" Black knew that you always asked for dough, even if it's not any—you never know.

"Ain't no money, kid. Took it all the last time," Ray said.

Black pulled the guy up from the kitchen floor. As Ray looked on, he took a hollow, sharp rod and jammed it into the guy's sternum and pushed it straight up to his aorta then slammed him down to the floor, his body now held up only by the kitchen cabinets.

They watched him sit there. Every time his heart beat, blood gushed out on the floor.

"In the closet . . . in the beige leather coat." Ray watched his cousin sit in a puddle of blood, life slowly draining from his body.

Dundee grabbed the coat and threw the money on the table.

Black grabbed the stacks. "Eighty thou. Come on, son, gots to be more—I got to eat." Black pulled out a syringe and needle and laid it on the table. He walked over to the kitchen. Dude was slumped over not moving.

Black grabbed the girl by her long, beautiful hair, snatching her up from the floor in one quick motion. Tears ran down her face, and her body trembled. He took her head and slammed it into one of the sharp edges of the wall. Blood poured down her face. He turned the stove on up high, still controlling her every movement by the grip he had on her hair, and pulled her face near the bright orange flame.

"It's the bag in the closet. That's it, man, my last. I'm done." Ray hung his head low.

"We know that, nigga." Lo bust him in the head with the butt of the gun.

Dundee opened the bag. "Bingo."

Black pushed the girl on the floor and grabbed the needle. "Hold him."

Lo hit his ass about four times with the gun and grabbed his arm. Black pushed the needle into his arm and squeezed.

Ray thought they were giving him heroin to kill him by overdose, but Black had pumped embalming fluid into his vein. "We out—don't leave no witnesses, Lo," Black said, headed for the front door.

Lo pulled a large Ginsu from the rack. And before the girl could move, he slammed the knife into her head and left it. She fell beside Ray, who was going crazy in a rage on the floor, bouncing around hollering.

They left out.

Black knew Ray was dead. The embalming fluid was going to flow through his bloodstream and burn every organ it hit. Black smiled. He knew they were done too.

Monica had her arms wrapped around Dee as he did one hundred miles per hour down 264 with a pack of bikes behind him. Dee hit the top of his helmet and began patting, and everybody slowed down to sixty while riding past the state troopers.

He patted Monica's hands to tell her to hold on, as he dropped the bike down into fourth gear. He gunned the gas, the RPM shot up, and he popped the clutch. Quickly, he got a tight hold of the grips as the front tire rose in the air and he did a wheelie down the interstate. When the front tire hit the ground he was running ninety. By this time the state troopers pulled out with their lights on.

He quickly punched it.

In a split second he was running one hundred and thirty with Monica's grip taking his breath. He saw the exit, broke it down, and exited on Interstate 44.

Once out the curve he punched it again. He knew once he hit Newtown Road he'd be home free. He saw exit 15B Newtown Road. *Yeah, got they muthafuckin' ass.* He patted Monica's hands to hold on.

Newtown exit was a sharp curve. He had to lean hard, but it meant nothing. He'd done this a thousand times.

He fell into the exit and leaned. The curve was sharp, and he leaned harder, adrenaline running. Dee felt Monica's body resisting; she was trying to lean the other way. The bike began to shake and at that moment Dee saw the gravel. Leaning hard, he tried to break it down, but it was no use. He was headed for the guardrail doing fifty. A split-second decision had to be made: Hold it and get wrapped up in the guardrail and bike or get the bike away from him.

He laid it down. As his body hit the hard, rugged road, he saw the bike crash and Monica's body hurl into the guardrail, breaking her neck and killing her instantly.

His body slammed into the rail, cutting his pelvis wide open and breaking his back. He lay in the street gasping for air, blood draining from his pelvis onto the road.

The other bikes stopped. Kev ran up and looked at Dee, his insides hanging out. Kev had to grab his stomach. Then he looked into Dee's eyes. "Come on, big bro, please hold on. You gonna be a'ight. Come on, Dee, Black need you. You can't leave Black. Come on."

Dee stared at Kev, and tears fell from both eyes. Then Dee forced a crooked smile and closed his eyes.

Kev picked up the phone and dialed Black.

"What's up, son?"

Kev didn't say anything. Nothing would come out.

"Kev, fuck you at? Me, Lo, and Dundee stuck in all this traffic on Newtown.

Kev wiped his eyes. "Dee just wrecked."

"What?" Black looked up and saw the ambulance and rescue squads trying to get to the exit. "Not in the exit?"

"Yeah. You see us?" Kev said.

"That's Dee, Lo. It's Dee." Black jumped out the car and ran across traffic, up the exit. He was outta breath, but he couldn't stop. "God, I know you wouldn't. I know you wouldn't. I know you wouldn't. I know you wouldn't." He saw Dee and collapsed beside his body. He tried to move, but his body was numb and he couldn't breathe.

Black's heart had dropped into his stomach. He wanted to die. He took Dee's head into his arm, hugged him, and cried.

Kev hugged Black and cried as the ambulance

and police came and moved them, placing the bodies in bags.

Black looked at the bike now torn to pieces. The picture of Junie was staring and didn't have a scratch. He looked into Junie's eyes and felt empty and alone. He walked over to Lo, who sat on the guardrail, his fist tight to his eyes.

They walked back down to the car in silence. Dundee drove to the restaurant. Black and Lo walked inside to the back.

The restaurant became silent when Moms let out a stabbing scream that only came with death. She held Black and squeezed him until he broke down again.

Tony walked to the front, his eyes bloodshot red from crying. Customers knew something was wrong. Tony turned off the sign and closed the store.

Mom, Auntie, Tony, Lo, and Black sat at the table in silence.

"It's time to start new—Virginia's been hard on us," Tony said.

"All of us," Black said. "All of us." He stood up and walked in the back. He stood at the back door looking into Lake Edward. What the fuck was he going to do. "Damn! Dee," he said out loud. "You wa'n' supposed to leave me like this." He couldn't stop his eyes from watering. This was the first time in his life that he was scared.